THE
HOLLYWOOD
SPIRAL

THE HOLLYWOOD SPIRAL

PAUL NEILAN

GRAND CENTRAL
PUBLISHING

NEW YORK   BOSTON

Grand Central Publishing
Hachette Book Group
1290 Avenue of the Americas, New York, NY 10104
grandcentralpublishing.com
twitter.com/grandcentralpub

First Edition: June 2021

Grand Central Publishing is a division of Hachette Book Group, Inc. The Grand Central Publishing name and logo is a trademark of Hachette Book Group, Inc.

The publisher is not responsible for websites (or their content) that are not owned by the publisher.

The Hachette Speakers Bureau provides a wide range of authors for speaking events. To find out more, go to www.hachettespeakersbureau.com or call (866) 376-6591.

Print book interior design by Sean Ford

Library of Congress Cataloging-in-Publication Data
Names: Neilan, Paul, author.
Title: The Hollywood spiral / Paul Neilan.
Description: First Edition. | New York : GCP, Grand Central Publishing, 2021.
Identifiers: LCCN 2020054035 | ISBN 9781538736678 (hardcover) | ISBN 9781538736661 (ebook)
Subjects: GSAFD: Science fiction.
Classification: LCC PS3614.E443 H65 2021 | DDC 813/.6--dc23
LC record available at https://lccn.loc.gov/2020054035

ISBNs: 978-1-5387-3667-8 (hardcover), 978-1-5387-3666-1 (ebook)

Printed in the United States of America

LSC-C

Printing 1, 2021

For Lily and Lucy and Avery and Quinn

THE
HOLLYWOOD
SPIRAL

FRIDAY

You want to hear a joke?"

I was sitting in an uncomfortable chair. The guy behind the desk had slicked-back hair and a mole under his left eye that was distracting me. It looked like a fly had landed on his face. Made a home for itself, burrowed into his skin. I couldn't help staring, waiting for it to twitch. My own cheek started to itch.

"Boss asked you a question," the big guy behind me said and flicked my ear hard with his finger.

"I'll take a joke," I said.

The guy behind the desk leaned forward on his elbows and showed me his teeth. "So this friend of mine's been going through a really rough time," he said. "Wife just left him, took the kids. My buddy's a wreck over it. He says to me the other night, he says, *Charlie, I don't know anymore. I don't know what to do. I just don't want to die alone.* So I shot him in the face. Ten times, emptied the clip. And I said to him, I said, *Does that make it any better, having somebody beside you when you go? Because it's kind of awkward for that other person. There's a big mess to clean up, I got no more bullets left. Just seems kind of selfish on your part, you know?* He didn't say anything but, I think he knew I was right."

The big guy behind me let out a giggle he'd been holding in, higher pitched than I was expecting. Like he'd been tickled with a feather and couldn't take it anymore.

"That's not bad," I said.

"What's the matter with you?" the big guy said, flicking my ear again. "You laugh when something's funny, dickhead."

"That's all right, Santos." The guy behind the desk sat back in his chair. He was in a sharp suit, a watch chain hanging from his vest. There was a dark screen on the wall behind him. "I do an open mic down at *Maxwells*. People there don't really get my sense of humor either."

He picked a speck of dust from his desk, blew it off his finger.

"See to me, shooting somebody in the face is hilarious," he said. "And you've got to be true to yourself onstage."

"You write what you know," I said.

"Exactly," he said, leaning forward. "My point exactly. You want a cigar?"

"I wouldn't mind," I said.

"That's nice," he said, opening the box of Cubans on his desk. "It's good to want things." He took one out, smelled it. Took his time lighting it for himself. I sat there as he puffed away. "Do you know who I am?" he said.

It was a little man's question. Doesn't matter who's asking or what the answer is.

"You're Charlie Horse," I said.

Santos smacked me so hard my flicked ear rang, nearly knocking me out of the chair.

"That's *Mr. Horschetti* to you," Santos said.

I looked at him over my shoulder. He gave me a gap-toothed grin.

"That's all right, Santos, we're all friends here," Charlie Horse said, working his cigar, rolling it in his fingers. "Ain't that right?"

He looked at me through the last puff of smoke. I didn't say anything.

"Good," Charlie Horse said, showing me his teeth again. "That's good. So us being so tight and all, how about you give me your fucking wallet."

"I use a clip," I said. I went to my pocket, tossed it onto his desk.

"Yeah, wallet's too bulky. You don't want to ruin the line of your pants. They cut those trousers for a reason . . . Harrigan," Charlie Horse said, looking over my license. "One forty-four Western Avenue, Number B. Sounds like a basement apartment."

"It is," I said.

"So I know who you are, and I know where you live," Charlie Horse said, taking the cash from my clip and tucking it into his vest pocket. "Now what brings an underground sack a shit like yourself into my fine establishment?"

I stretched my legs, settled into the chair as best I could.

"I'm not above slumming," I said. "On occasion."

"I don't know anybody who is," he said, patting his pocket. "So I'll ask you again. What the fuck you doing in my club?"

"Same as anybody, Charlie," I said. "I'm looking for a girl."

"Not just any girl. You're looking for Anna," he said, spitting another cloud of smoke at me. "Yeah, that's right. I already know. There's no secrets in this joint. Not from me."

He chewed his cigar, took it out of his mouth, considered it. I watched the smoke drift up, hover around a sprinkler head above us.

"Takes heat to set the system off," Charlie Horse said, following my eyes. "Smoke's fine. So tell me, Harrigan. Who you working for?"

"I don't talk business, Charlie. Not even with my friends," I said. "I'm sure you understand."

I braced for another smack. Felt a gun against the back of my head instead.

"Oh, I understand completely," Charlie Horse said, picking another speck of dust from his desk. "And I respect your discretion. I really do. But Santos here, not so much."

Santos pushed the barrel forward until my head was bowed.

"Don't make me ask you again, Harrigan," Charlie Horse said.

I wasn't scared the way he wanted me to be. The angle was off. If Santos pulled the trigger he would've splashed my brains all over his boss's desk. Charlie Horse wouldn't like that.

"What've we got here, Santos?" he said. "A guy who knows how to keep his mouth shut? That's a rare thing, Harrigan. Like my cousin's albino Weimaraner. A rare and stupid thing."

Santos took the gun off me. I looked up to see Charlie Horse grinning.

"I remember you," he said, jabbing his cigar at me. "You're the Harrigan used to run with Clyde Faraday's crew."

"Long time ago," I said.

"Long time," Charlie Horse said, puffing on his cigar. "Shame about what happened to old Clyde, huh? Ending up in a place like that."

He searched my face. I wasn't sure what he was looking for, how well I'd hidden it. I could hear Santos breathing behind me.

"You should've seen it, Santos, back in the old days," he said. "Before Zodiac. Before Grid. Out running the streets, the pool halls, the rackets. You were either a bitch or a butcher, there was no in-between. Like the Wild West, all over the city."

"And we were the Indians," I said.

"Don't sell yourself short, Harrigan," Charlie Horse said. "I'll do it for you. You were a fucking buffalo, at best."

"Good one, boss," Santos said, giggling.

"That's all over now," Charlie Horse said, almost wistful. He straightened his cuff links, one after the other. "It's a new world out there. But not in here. We still go by the old rules in my house. I stock real girls, none of that hologram hybrid shit. We play real games, no simulates. So let me tell you how it is."

He stubbed his cigar out in the ashtray.

"You work for me now, Harrigan," he said. "You're gonna find Anna. You're gonna bring me my fucking Danish."

"I'm no bounty hunter," I said. "I don't take people in."

"You are what I say you are. And you do what I tell you to do. Remember that." He tossed my empty money clip back at me. "Now get the fuck out of here."

Santos lifted me by the scruff of my neck and shoved me towards the door. Rammed my forehead into the wood as he opened it.

"And Harrigan," Charlie Horse said, fingers tented in front of him. I could barely make him out through the blur. "Don't you let me down. I hate it when my friends let me down."

THURSDAY

I met Stan Volga just after he'd fallen down a flight of stairs.

I was sitting at my table, drinking cheap champagne in the middle of the day when I saw a pair of legs pinwheel down the steps out the window. There was a thud, like a bag of garbage hitting the sidewalk after being thrown off a roof. Then silence.

I took a long drink and listened until I could hear the rain again. I thought about who might be dead on my doorstep, who I'd miss most if they were. I was still thinking when I heard a knock on the door.

He was standing there in a rumpled suit two sizes too big, a thin mustache over his lip. There was a nasty lump on his forehead, already starting to swell.

"Are you Harrigan?" he said.

"Are you bleeding?" I said.

He looked up the stone steps to the street. Felt around on himself like he was trying to find his keys.

"I don't think so," he said.

"Probably just a skull fracture," I said. "You'll be fine."

"I don't have an appointment," he said.

"That's all right," I said. "I'm not a doctor."

I was closing the door when he said, "Wait. Wait! Eddie Lompoc sent me!"

I knew Eddie from those circles you run in when you're rounding the drain. He had bug eyes and a bad habit of rubbing the spot where his chin should've been when he was trying to cheat you at cards. I worked with him in Clyde Faraday's old gang, a lifetime ago, before it all went south. I hadn't seen him in months. I didn't miss him.

"He said you can help me," he said.

"I don't do that kind of thing anymore," I said.

"But I haven't even told you what it's about," he said.

"Let's keep it that way," I said.

I went to shut the door again and he jammed his foot in, pressed his face into the gap.

"Please," he said. His mustache was wet, eyelids fluttering. "Can you just, please?"

I never could stand it, seeing a man beg. I moved aside and he came in veering to the left like the floor was tilting on him. He overcorrected and swung to the right, then stopped with both hands out like it was his first time on a surfboard and he saw sharks in the water. It cost him some effort to get steady, before he looked around the room.

There was a fern in the corner. A big map of the world I'd hung to hide the water damage on the wall. A half-empty bottle of champagne was sweating it out on the table.

"Champagne!" he said, way too excited when he saw it. "What's the occasion?"

I'd gotten a rent-past-due notice on my door that morning. The second one this month. But I wasn't being evicted. Not yet anyway. It seemed like enough. You could die of thirst waiting for a reason.

"You tell me," I said. "You look like you've been celebrating."

"No," he said, going serious. "Not celebrating. Drowning."

He lurched towards the wall, stopped with his face inches from the map.

"There it is," he said, slurring. "The motherland. Denmark."

He didn't sound like he was from Denmark. He sounded piss drunk or severely concussed or both.

"So cold," he said, stroking the map with his index finger. "So beautiful, but so very cold."

He put his face closer, inhaled through his nose, settled his cheek against it like a soft pillow.

"I'll get you some ice for that forehead," I said.

I didn't want him passing out on me. I went to the kitchenette, dumped some cubes in a bag. When I came back he was sitting at my table with the champagne bottle in his hand.

He tipped it back, took a gulp.

"Help yourself," I said, whipping the bag at him. It hit him in the chest and fell rattling, spilling ice cubes in his lap. He looked down at them, then at the champagne in his hand. Puzzled through it like a word problem on a test he hadn't studied for before he took an ice cube off his pants and plopped it in his mouth, held the bottle to his forehead.

"Thanks," he said, crunching the ice.

"What's your name?" I said.

"Stan Volga," he said.

"Why are you here, Stan?" I said.

"We should have a toast," he said.

He chewed the ice like candy before he swallowed it.

"To Anna," Stan Volga said solemnly, raising the bottle. "Always to Anna."

He popped himself in the nose before he found his mouth. Then he fumbled in his oversized suit jacket, pulled out a Polaroid and handed it across the table to me.

You see the same faces, everywhere you go. When you've been around long enough, everyone reminds you of someone else. Not this girl. She was all her own. She had blond hair, so blond it was almost white. Blue eyes you could pick out of a lineup. She wasn't smiling. From the tilt of her chin she looked like a praying mantis about to bite someone's head off. I could think of worse ways to go.

"Eddie Lompoc said you can find people," Stan Volga said.

I was going to find Eddie Lompoc, tell him to keep his mouth shut. That's how it happens, somebody talking. That's all it takes for Zodiac to catch the scent. I was still staring at the picture.

"That's my Anna," Stan Volga said.

He took another gulp of champagne, set the bottle on

the table. Turned the gold wedding band on his finger like he was cracking an empty safe.

"She drinks vodka like a Russian but I've never seen her drunk," he said. "She talks in her sleep, screams in Danish but won't tell me what any of it means. She's the only one who really understands me."

The girl who finally gets you, and you can't follow a word of her explanation. Seemed like the only way it could work.

"What's her last name?" I said.

"I don't know," he said.

Pretty much ruled her out as the wife.

"Where did you two meet?" I said.

"I don't remember," he said, looking down at the ice in his lap.

"How long has she been missing?" I said.

"I'm not sure," he said. "I haven't seen her in two days."

"Go to the police," I said.

Stan Volga shook his head. "I'm trying to keep it quiet," he said. "Off Grid."

Off Grid. That's what brought him to me. Eddie Lompoc knew I stayed away from Zodiac, kept to my own side of the street. Like that mattered anymore. Like the city hadn't changed on me. Still thinking I could get by on my own. Eddie probably figured I'd be desperate enough to bite. I couldn't say he was wrong.

Stan Volga reached for the champagne bottle, avoiding my eyes. Ice cubes spilled to the floor like spent shells. "Eddie Lompoc said you could find her," he said.

"Tell Eddie—" I stopped. I'd tell him myself. "That's not

how it works, Stan. I'm not in the business anymore. Even if I was, you need something to go on. Something more than this."

I waved the Polaroid at him. But I didn't give it back.

"I can pay," Stan Volga said, reaching inside his jacket, pulling out a roll of bills. "Cash."

That, that was something.

I was lying to Stan Volga. It's not hard to track someone down. Most people can't wait to tell you where they are, where they've been, where they're headed next. They're desperate to be discovered. They can't wait to be found. That's why they're on Grid.

But once you start looking, you can be found too. They tell you it's good for you. Helps your Score every time you check in. What they don't say is every search is logged, recorded and scrutinized by Zodiac. Your interests and inquiries leave their own trail like bread crumbs, leading right back to you. You're better off not giving them an excuse to look into it.

I showed Stan Volga the door and I plugged into Grid. I used a dummy profile, rerouted through a subfloor where I could skip the simulations and commercials, all the noise, and ran facial recognition on the Polaroid. I sifted the caches and the unmined stacks, the cracks and corners in the system where information pretends to hide.

An hour later I had nothing. That was unusual. Everyone

leaves a trace of themselves, whether they like it or not. Everybody's got a ghost on Grid. Even me. Not this Anna. She was nowhere.

Maybe I was rusty. It didn't feel like it. There was more to it than that. Something about Anna I couldn't place. That didn't fit. I needed some background. I went to the source.

Delia was a street kid when I met her, telling fortunes on the Strip, picking pockets when she could to make a living. Even then she had a look that could crack you wide open, so easy you weren't sure if you'd given away all your secrets or she'd lifted them from you. She had the second sight, the third eye, all the stories in her deck of tarot cards. She also had a line to every doorman, hotel clerk, and bartender in the city. When they came in to get their palms read they'd tell her everything they knew.

She'd tipped me off once that a hired gun named Jimmy Fitz was asking around town for me. I'd owed her ever since. No matter how long between visits she was never surprised to see me. Like she was always expecting it, like she knew.

I took a walk up Normandie in the rain to a dilapidated strip mall on the corner of Fountain. On the second floor, in between a bail bond and a Burmese takeout, the sign above the door read ∴ with a yellow light behind it. A bell jangled as I went through the door.

There was a round card table in the middle of the room draped with a green velvet tablecloth, a mobile of silvered wire ellipses suspended above it like halos orbiting at estranged angles. An altar sat in the corner, candles stacked on wax-strewn shelves, framed by feathered wings. Circular mirrors hung on the walls opposite each other, their reflections stretching to infinity. I caught sight of myself in the cross fire. Every one of me needed a shave.

"Harrigan," Delia said as she came through a curtain of beads along the far wall. "Long time no see."

She had a gold hoop in her nose and a tattoo snaking up her right arm of that painting by Klimt, *Death and Life*, all the sleeping people huddled together as a skeleton watches like it's waiting to devour them whole.

"How you been, Delia?" I said.

"Busy," she said. "Half the city's lost their mind with this comet coming. The other half's looking for it. I'm cleaning up on both sides."

I looked at her.

"The comet?" Delia said. "The one passing directly over us next weekend? Brahe's Reckoning? Next Sunday? At midnight?"

I didn't say anything.

"People are freaking out, Harrigan. Where've you been?" she said, shaking her head. "Forget it, I'll find out. Have a seat."

She lit a candle on the altar in the corner, blew it out, lit it again.

"I'm not here for a reading," I said as she sat down.

"But you're getting one anyway," Delia said. "It's almost like fate, huh?"

She nodded to the empty chair, pulled a purple-lined case from beneath the table and unpacked her implements. A deck of cards. A crystal decanter, half filled with rain water. A mason jar of weed. A squat, tea kettle glass bong. A wooden lighter with a Celtic knot emblazoned on the side.

She drained the decanter into the bong. Unscrewed the mason jar, the dank scent mingling with the sandalwood and jasmine already floating around us.

"This is Morrigan's Dream," she said, holding up a goldflecked bud like a jewel. "We're all just passing through."

She sparked the lighter. Smoke swirled in the glass and climbed the neck of the tea kettle in a rush as she inhaled. She nodded to me and I cut the deck of cards before her. Then she exhaled, smoke crawling over the green velvet table, clinging like mist.

"Now," she said, instantly serene. "Let's begin."

She turned the first card.

"The Devil," she said, flame rimming the leering face on the card. "The Demon."

"Hell of a way to start," I said.

"We don't know as much about him as we think we do," she said. "*Lucifer* means 'light bringer.'"

Her pupils expanded. Her face took on a subtle slant.

"I was too big for the Bible," she said, a smile flitting quick across her lips and disappearing. "They had me slither in the Garden and tempt the usurper in the desert. Bit parts for the Morning Star. But they left my story to be told by a blind man, in fucking English. Blasphemy."

She raised her left hand, two fingers and thumb extended.

"Give me the sophistry of Greek," she said. "The fire of Aramaic. The forked tongue of Babylon."

She closed her eyes, let her head tip back.

"Babylon," she whispered again as the halos above us converged, tracing a conical shape in the air, a glittering tornado that immediately dispersed.

She turned the next card.

"The Paladin," she said, a figure on horseback, armored in chain mail. "A knight errant. A knight of faith. Charged by their code, cast by their quest. Theirs is a calling. Theirs the response. Theirs the calamity ensuing."

Her head swung back and forth. She touched the tattoo on her shoulder.

"Sorry for that last bit," she said. "That was still the Devil talking. Once he gets going it's hard to shut him up."

She turned the last card.

"The Fool," she said, the jester in a belled cap, dancing, arms in the air.

"Him I've met," I said.

"You've met them all, Harrigan. And you will again," she said. "The trick is remembering what they tell you, when they show themselves to you."

"What about him," I said, pointing to the card. "What's he got to say?"

"He's a tough one," she said, staring at the Fool. "She'll do anything for a laugh. Say what he has to, be who she must. A smoke and a joke, a juggle and a mug. But they've got a blade in their belt, same as anyone else."

"I'll keep that in mind," I said.

"That's two hundred for the reading," Delia said, replacing the cards and shuffling the deck. "Unless there was something else."

I pushed some of Stan Volga's money across the table, along with the Polaroid.

"She's pretty," Delia said, looking her over. "What's her name?"

"Anna," I said. "She's Danish."

"You stalking her for yourself or someone else?" she said to me.

"I haven't decided yet," I said. "Ever seen her around?"

"No," she said. "Her I'd remember."

She thought for a second, made up her mind.

"There's a place on Argyle called *Lekare*. Corner of Selma," she said. "It's a character's club. Might be her kind of crowd."

"What's a character's club?" I said.

"Same as anywhere," Delia said, smiling sort of wearily as she folded the bills I'd given her. "Everybody's playing someone else."

It had been raining all week, all month, all year. The water rushed in a gully down the street to the backed-up sewer grates, clogged with garbage, leaving every intersection a fetid reservoir. I followed the sidewalk as the robo cabs rolled past, silent and sentient, running their routes. Stayed under the overhangs where I could find them, kept my head down. Turned my face from the Zodiac cams on every corner. They were always watching. Didn't mean you had to make it easy for them.

I saw a hooded figure coming towards me, a long gray robe glistening like seal skin under the streetlight. As they passed a hand held out a pamphlet. I took it, watched them recede, dragging a gray garbage can behind them. I looked at the pamphlet.

Are you ready to begin again?

Free the selves. Unveil the self.

fvrst chvrch mvlTverse

There is no I. There is no U.

All r welcome. All r 1.

6765 Franklin Avenue.

I pocketed the pamphlet, kept going. Went over the freeway with its traffic clotted underneath. I turned on Argyle, walked the Selma block twice before I found it, after two spindly kids came out through a hidden door in a wall of blacked-out glass.

"*Lekare?*" I said to one of them, his face smeared white with powder.

He hissed at me, showed me his vampire fangs under his too-long bangs as the other one wrapped his arms around his chest, holding him back in a loose embrace.

"Not here," he said, licking the side of his pale face. "Not yet, my pet." He stretched a crooked finger to the glass. "*Lekare*, if you are willing." He licked his face again.

I left them on the sidewalk to howl at the moon, went through the glass door into a black light and a twitching strobe, figures moving like spiders all around me. I made my way past replicants and droogs, a cemetery Dorothy in onyx shoes. A clutch of space pirates were slung on low couches, sucking on a hookah. A strung-out Snow White and a derelict Alice both leaned against a statuesque Carmen Miranda, withered fruit piled high on her head, cheeks blue like she'd been left out in the cold.

I went to the bar, where things made more sense.

The bartender had torn angel's wings and a black eye. She poured me a double and I left a big tip. Sat there a while before I showed her the Polaroid of Anna. Her eyes glazed over before she shook her head, moved down the bar.

I watched the room behind me in the mirror over the top-shelf bottles as it showed in freeze-frame strobe flashes.

It was giving me a headache. I was halfway through my second drink when somebody leaned into my ear.

"Do you like this music?" he said.

He was in a black vinyl trench coat with Wellington boots, a Polaroid camera around his neck.

"It's all right," I said.

From the speaker above a woman was wailing like she was plummeting to her death while some robots smacked a synth with hammers.

"They are *Vektor*," he said, leaning into my ear again. "She is a ghost on a ledge, haunted by technology."

There was a halt in his voice, a slight hitch. He was from somewhere else, but I couldn't place it. Maybe Denmark.

"I know the feeling," I said. "You take a lot of pictures?" I nodded at the camera.

"It is a passion of mine," he said. "One of many."

He puckered his lips at me.

"I hold the photo between my fingers as it develops," he said, flittering his hands in the air like palsied butterflies. "I never shake it. *Never*. It is important to touch—to feel—as it blossoms in my hand."

The tip of his tongue darted like he was licking a crumb from the corner of his mouth. He left it there, peeking out. A half-eaten slug, trying to escape.

"You take this one?" I said.

I showed him the picture of Anna. He looked it over, pulled his tongue back in.

"I take so many," he said, backing away from me, dragging his fingers over his face like veils. "Who can know?"

He danced around as he backpedaled before disappearing into the crowd. I looked for him in the mirror, didn't see him again. Didn't feel like following, wherever he went.

I finished my drink, headed to the bathroom. The fluorescent lights overhead were too bright and too steady after the twitching strobe, the floor too filthy. I stood at the urinal, waited for my head to clear.

I heard the door open behind me, the harsh music swelling, then choking off again as it closed.

When I turned there were three of them, blocking the door. The one in the middle had a blond mohawk, so blond it was almost white. Blue eyes like a husky and a studded black leather band up his forearm. The other two were in black leather pants with too many zippers. Torn T-shirts ripped into scars, sutured with safety pins.

I went to the sink, washed my hands. Took my time drying them.

I watched them in the mirror. They hadn't moved.

When I went to slide past the blond one put his hand on my chest, pushed me back.

"You go nowhere," the blond one said, the same hitch in his voice as the Polaroid guy. "It is very late for you."

"What's this about, fellas?" I said, as the other two fanned out, flanking me.

They didn't say anything. My hands were out. My back was to the wall.

It's never a fair fight. That's what makes it a fight.

When the blond one took a step towards me I dropped my shoulder, hit him in the jaw as hard as I could. He staggered back, still blocking the door. I turned to the one on the left just in time for him to punch me square in the face. My head snapped back and the light changed like he'd knocked off my sunglasses. I wasn't wearing any. I kept my legs beneath me, caught him with a hook before the other one crumpled me with a kidney shot. I bent and the blond one wrangled me into a headlock, jerking at my neck, choking me before I rammed my hand up between his legs and crushed, then twisted.

"Mine testikler!" he cried.

It echoed off the grimed walls as I broke free, but before I could straighten up they hit me from either side, knocking me to the floor. I was on my hands and knees when one of them kicked me in the ribs, rolling me over until I was sitting up against the stall, dazed. The one closest leaned down and mashed his hand into my crotch as I sat there, baffled.

"I took his testikler as well," he said, showing the others his open hand, evening a score that really didn't need to be settled.

"Well done, Sig," the blond one said. "Tor?"

"He has had enough, Brand," the one against the far wall said, his eyes soft.

Brand stood over me, smirking. "You will know trembling. You will know pain. You will know fear," he said, running his hands through his mohawk. "Brahe's Reckoning is upon you. The past rises to devour you whole. Los Angeles will fall. The beast is awoken. The hour is nigh."

"Nothing good about that," I said.

Brand reached his hand out to me and flame leapt from his leather armband. I ducked under the fireball as it scorched the wall of the stall.

"Tell Charlie Horse, Anna works for him no longer," Brand said. "Soon none ever will again. Quite soon. Very quite. The end has come for all of you."

I sat there as they filed out, one after the other. Brand first, Sig following. Tor, the one with the soft eyes, looked back at me as the door closed.

I picked myself up off the floor, looked in the mirror for a while. Spit some blood into the sink.

FRIDAY

Why didn't you tell me she's a hooker?" I said.

"Anna's not a hooker, she's a hostess," Stan Volga said, sitting at my table. "It's about companionship, not sex."

People said the same thing about cocker spaniels. I didn't believe them either.

"You met her at *Fatales*," I said.

Stan Volga looked down into his glass. His hand shook as he lifted it, took a gulp. He was ragged when he came in, wearing the same suit as the day before. He had that wobble in his eyes, the one you get at the tail end of a bender, right before you hit the skid. A drink helps. I was having one myself.

"How much do you owe?" I said.

He looked at me. "Owe?" he said. "I don't owe anybody anything."

"You ever heard of Charlie Horschetti?" I said.

Stan Volga shook his head.

"They call him Charlie Horse," I said.

He'd made his name blowing peoples' kneecaps off whenever they owed him money or looked at him funny or for no special reason at all. Or maybe his name had made him. It was hard to say which came first. Nobody cares about chickens or eggs when they're hopping around on a prosthetic leg.

"*Fatales* is his place," I said.

"Does he know where Anna is?" Stan Volga said.

"She doesn't work there anymore," I said.

"Well maybe he knows where she went!" he said, getting excited. "I'll go with you. I'm not afraid of any—"

"You're not going anywhere, Stan," I said. "Neither am I."

"What?" he said, spilling half his drink down his chest. "But we have to. You have to find her. Eddie Lompoc said—"

"Eddie Lompoc likes to run his mouth," I said. "So do you."

He looked at me for as long as he could stand it before turning away. "What's that supposed to mean?" he said quietly.

"I asked you where you met Anna when you came in yesterday," I said. "You told me you didn't know. What else aren't you telling me, Stan?"

He smoothed the front of his stained, wrinkled jacket, took another drink.

"I'm sorry," he said, fingering his wedding ring. "I'm sorry I didn't tell you. I was embarrassed." He looked at the table, brought his watery eyes up again. "I know how it sounds, falling for a hostess. I know it's stupid. I know that's what you think. But it's different with Anna. It is. I haven't felt this way since—"

He looked away, dragged his hands over his face like he was shuffling a deck with all the good cards missing.

"You have to find her," he said, his voice small. "Eddie Lompoc said you would."

"Go home, Stan," I said. "Sleep it off. Or start it up again. Either way, go home."

He reached inside his jacket, came out with another wad of bills. Smaller than the day before, but it was still a roll. "Take it," he said, laying it on the table. "Take all of it. Just find her."

His chin was quivering. He couldn't meet my eyes.

"Anna's all that matters," Stan Volga said.

He was holding out on me. They always do. There's always more. It's always worse.

I looked at the money like I was thinking about it, but I didn't need to. I already knew where I was headed.

I walked down Hollywood Boulevard the wrong way in the rain. Away from the Strip and the stars in the sidewalk. Towards the ragged end where the street people in blue tarps huddled in doorways and camped under disused bus stops. I walked past the hourly motels with bars on their windows, their flashing signs—*The Starlet, The Big Break, The Afterglow*—scripted in neon that dripped onto the sidewalk and puddled in the gutter like spilled dreams. I walked past the girls on the corners, their shimmering short dresses, spinning like disco balls unraveling. Past the old park with the crumbling Frank Lloyd Wright house, its ruin still scaffolded, another Zodiac renovation never begun—not on this side of town—now a shooting gallery for climbers. All of it passing by until I saw the lurid red sign for *Fatales*, 4181 Hollywood Boulevard.

I went through the door. Waved the coat check girl off before I took the body scan. Then through a curtain, around a curve in the wall that opened to the main room. Cards and dice were set up along the far wall under spotlights. A few suits rolling, all of them losing. There was a bar along the opposite wall with cocktail tables scattered in between—candles flickering in red globes with the lights down—where guys were sitting close to girls in sheer teddies and negligees, all of them wearing heels to the same slumber party. The girls threw their heads back, laughing, mismatched couples holding hands across the table as they drank.

I stood there, taking it in. The septic tank beauty, subterranean and full of shit. Without it the whole town would stop running.

I felt a hand on my arm. Soft fingers, trailing.

"Do you play?" she said.

She had long black hair pulled over her shoulder, hiding one of her dark eyes.

"Not if I can help it," I said.

"Shall we take a mark on the tables?" she said. "They'll stake you, if you prefer."

"I just got here," I said. "I'm easing into it."

"I like a man who takes his time," she said, smiling up at me. "Would you sit with me?"

I told her I would.

She led me to a table in the middle. I watched another couple stand from nearby and disappear through the long red curtain in the back.

"What's your name?" she said as we sat down.

"Harrigan," I said.

"I'm Aoki," she said. "Do you like champagne, Harrigan?"

"I do," I said.

"Shall we have a bottle?" she said.

"Let's start with a glass," I said. "See where that takes us."

She smiled, raised two fingers. The bubbles floated over on a silver tray.

"You've never been here before," Aoki said as the girl set the tall glasses down before us.

"How can you tell?" I said.

"I can always tell," she said, looking into my eyes as she raised her glass. "To our first time together."

She tipped her head back slightly, hair still masking half her face.

"You're not like the others," she said.

"Why's that?" I said.

"You haven't started talking yet," she said. "Most men can't wait to get going. They've got so much to say."

"What's behind the curtain?" I said, looking to the back wall.

She smiled, combed her hands through her hair.

"That's better," she said. "We can have more privacy back there. Our own room where we can relax, get to know each other. Would you like that, Harrigan?"

"I'm good here," I said. "For now."

She sat back, crossed her legs. She was wearing a long white dress shirt, loosely buttoned so her collar bone showed. Her heels laced up her calves, slender strictures. She took a drink.

"Do you live around here?" Aoki said.

"Not too far," I said.

"What do you do?" she said.

"Not too much," I said.

"Why not?" she said.

"I was in the business for a while," I said. "I got out."

"What made you leave?" she said.

"It was time," I said.

"I know what that's like," she said, taking another drink. I took one myself.

"Is Anna working tonight?" I said.

"Who?" Aoki said.

"Anna," I said. "Danish girl. Blonde."

"What's the matter?" she said. "I'm not enough for you?"

She was playing wounded, but she'd given me a subtle shake of her head. It was quick, but I caught it.

"You're plenty." I drained my champagne. "How about we have another glass and you tell me all about yourself?" I said.

"What do you want to know?" she said, cocking her head as she raised her two fingers.

Before I could answer a meaty hand came down on my shoulder. I saw a gold signet ring with the image of a bull on one of the thick fingers. Taurus. Zodiac. I looked up into the face of a bruiser in a maroon dinner jacket with a head like a canned ham. His nose had been flattened. Two cauliflower ears stuck out on either side.

"You want to come with me," the big guy said.

"I'm fine where I am," I said.

"I wasn't asking," he said.

Aoki dropped her eyes as I stood from the table.

"It was nice meeting you," I said before he pushed me away, through a curtain behind one of the craps tables. We went down a long hallway that ended at a heavy wooden door.

"What's this about?" I said as he knocked twice and opened it. Shoved me through.

I stumbled into a wide office with a leather couch along the wall, a guy with slicked-back hair sitting behind the desk. The big guy sat me down in an uncomfortable chair. The guy behind the desk looked at me and said "You want to hear a joke?"

SATURDAY

"That's the thing about champagne," Clyde Faraday said, the first time I sat across a table from him, all those years ago. "It doesn't have to be the good stuff. If it's got bubbles, it's good enough."

He savored a long swallow.

"There's a lesson in there somewhere, if you want to learn it," he said. "But you don't, do you kid. Not yet."

I took a drink.

"You know how to handle a gun," he said. "That much was obvious when you pulled it on me. But it's not enough."

"I do all right," I said.

"Stick-up jobs on street corners only take you so far," he said. "And it's not any place you want to stay. How long you been in town?"

"Long enough," I said.

"Not yet you haven't, kid. Not yet," he said. "If you want

to survive in this racket you need people. Somebody looking out for you. A crew."

"I can take care of myself," I said.

"Can you? You'd be the first," he said. "I'm offering you an opportunity. They don't come around often. This one won't pass your way again. What do you say?"

We had history, me and Clyde Faraday. Not all of it bad. That was more than I could say about most people. It ended wrong, like it always does, but it wasn't over. Not yet.

I made a few calls, found out what Charlie Horse meant when he said it was a shame, old Clyde ending up in a place like this. I sat in the small room, a crepe shade pulled over the narrow window, and listened to the machines. An accordion valve compressed and expanded above the bed, sighing with every shallow breath. The steady drip from an IV marked time as a bag full of clear liquid slowly drained. The jarring beeps of a heart monitor squealed, scrawling its inscrutable line across the monitor. It played like a doomed symphony, the savage susurrus of sickness, end stage.

He had a tube in his arm, a magnetic clip on his finger. Wires attached to his chest. His hair had gone white at the temples. His face was pale, but not sallow. He hadn't lost his jaw. Even flat on his back in a hospice bed, he was still Clyde Faraday.

Clyde's eyelids rustled. I leaned forward in the chair and he opened both eyes, looked at me strange and vacant. Like he was staring into a clouded pond, trying to see bottom.

"Clyde," I said as he lay there. "It's me. Harrigan."

His eyes didn't register the name. Or anything else.

It was too late. I was too late. Clyde Faraday was gone.

I wanted to stand up. Walk out. Never come back. I knew how. I'd done it before.

His eyes didn't move as I got out of the chair.

"Good seeing you, Clyde," I said. "Take care."

"When I was a year old, my parents found me under the Christmas tree, eating dog crap with a spoon," Clyde Faraday said, his voice monotone. "It wasn't even our dog."

"Whose dog was it?" I said.

"The neighbor's basset hound," Clyde said. "We were watching him while they were on vacation. His name was Baxter. And instead of calling an ambulance or shooting the dog or just cleaning me up and never, ever mentioning it again, my parents grabbed a video camera and started recording. The part where I dropped the spoon and smeared dog shit all over my face with my tiny hands was dramatic, but the real climax came when Baxter wandered into the frame and howled at the ceiling as I clapped like the happy child I would never again be, splattering crap all over myself before giving the camera a shitty grin."

A cloud passed over his face. A lengthening shadow.

"We watched that tape every Christmas," Clyde said. "Whenever anybody came by the house. My parents would pull people in off the street—carolers, neighbors out making snowmen with their kids, fucking Jehovah's Witnesses—so they could all gather round the TV and glance at me uncomfortably as they laughed in horror and disgust. They showed it to everybody. My father even played it for the first girl I ever brought home, even though I begged him not to. Later, when I tried to kiss her good night she took off screaming, whipping her head around and waving her arms like she was being swarmed by bees. It was a long, long time before I found another girlfriend, and she wasn't pretty at all."

The machine attached to the tube in his arm began beeping steadily, louder and louder. I wasn't sure what any of it meant.

"After years of talking about it, my dad finally sent the tape in to one of those *Funniest Videos* shows," Clyde said. "The ones that ran home movies of people getting hit in the nuts with Wiffle ball bats and falling down drunk at weddings. But he waited until I was a senior in high school to do it. That's when I was shown, in prime time across the nation, laughing in a diaper as I ate dog shit. We didn't win any money, and I didn't go to my prom. The things they wrote in my yearbook were unspeakably filthy."

Clyde's hands were folded tightly in his lap, a clenched and squandered prayer.

"I've always understood why people get depressed around the holidays," Clyde said. "But I could never figure out why there weren't more suicides."

"Hello, Mr. Clyde!" a lady in floral print scrubs said as she stood in the doorway. "Time for your medicine!"

"I'll get out of your way," I said, moving aside.

"Is OK," she said, swapping out the bag of clear fluid and checking the IV in his arm. "Only take a minute."

She pressed a button on the machine and Clyde closed his eyes. When he opened them he looked right at me and said, "Harrigan. What are you doing here?"

"I could ask you the same thing," I said.

"I'm fucking dying is what I'm doing," Clyde said.

"Mr. Clyde," the lady said, clucking her tongue.

"There she is. There's my Rosalita," Clyde said. "Anybody ever tell you you put the spice in *hospice*?"

She smiled, shook her head as she raised the crepe window shade and left the room.

"Sit down, Harrigan," Clyde said. "I don't like people standing over me. Feels like a fucking funeral. How long you been here?"

"Not long," I said.

"I say anything?" he said, uncertain.

"Not a word," I said.

"This medicine," he said, looking up at the clear plastic bag. "It gives me *windows of lucidity*. The rest of the time I'm out of my fucking mind."

"I'm the same with whiskey," I said.

"So tell me kid, what did I miss?" he said.

"You tell me," I said, looking up at the machines. "What's the story here, Clyde?"

"What does it matter," he said. "Place like this, everybody knows how it ends."

He looked away, out the narrow window.

"How'd you know I was in here?" he said.

"Charlie Horse said something about it," I said. "I did some asking around."

"Charlie Horse?" Clyde said. "What are you doing with that punk?"

"Job went sideways," I said. "You know how it goes."

"I thought you were done with all that, Harrigan," he said.

"I was," I said. "I am."

"It's not done with you though, huh?" he said. "That was your mistake. Thinking you had a choice. Thinking it was yours to make."

"I'm not here to apologize," I said.

"Neither am I," Clyde said.

There was a hard light in his eyes. Like a barrel fire under an overpass in winter. I watched it fade as his face softened, went slack at the edges, until he was looking through me again. There was a muted screen on the wall playing an old game show. *Wheel of Fortune.*

The screen in my pocket vibrated.

Can you meet me at The Sinking Ship in an hour? It's Aoki.

I sat there, waited for Clyde's eyes to close. It wasn't long.

The Sinking Ship was a bar on Fairfax with rippling blue walls and an uneven wood floor that sloped and dipped like a listing schooner. There were framed newspaper pages lamenting the *Titanic* and the *Lusitania* and a life preserver over the door stamped "HMS *Hood.*" Oil paintings were hung slightly crooked at haphazard heights showing a harpooned whale in anguish smashing a clipper ship in half and a pirate ship on fire, its crow's nest ablaze as it sank beneath the waves.

Aoki was in a booth at the back, away from the porthole windows. I almost didn't recognize her in her ripped jeans and olive drab jacket, hair piled under a slouching knit hat. I could see both her dark eyes. They told me nothing as I sat down.

The painting over our booth showed three girls in diaphanous drapery, sprawled and singing on the shore as a ship full of sailors dashed themselves on the rocks.

"Get you something?" the bartender said.

Aoki had a fishbowl glass of sangria in front of her, blood red and thick with soaked fruit.

"I'll have one of those," I said.

He nodded, walked away. There was nobody else in the bar.

"What do you want with Anna?" Aoki said.

"How did you get my number?" I said.

"You told me your name, Harrigan," she said.

"That's not enough," I said.

I'd made sure of that. She took a drink as the bartender came back with my glass, speared an orange wedge with her straw, picked it clean.

"The body scan," she said finally, after the bartender walked away. "It gave up your profile."

"Body scan," I said. "Everybody who goes into *Fatales* gets screened?"

"Stripped and searched," she said. "Everything they've got on Grid. Some of what they don't show there too."

It was a breach. Zodiac had strict protection protocols in place. Formal data regulations giving everyone their imaginary privacy, all of it informally enforced. But there were ways around them if you knew what you were doing.

Charlie Horse had found one. What he used it for was another question.

"They didn't have much on you, but it was enough," Aoki said. "So why are you looking for Anna?"

"A guy by the name of Stan Volga asked me to find her," I said. "Thin mustache, sloppy drunk. Looks like he sleeps in his suit."

She shook her head. "Anna's got a lot of regulars," she said.

"She make a habit of shaking them down?" I said.

Aoki looked at me, took a drink from her fishbowl. Cast her eyes at the bartender, idly polishing a glass. She leaned over the table.

"It's what we do," she said. "*Fatales* is wired. The whole place. The tables, the back rooms. If we meet a client after hours, Charlie picks the spot, sets it up. It's all screened, all recorded."

"Blackmail," I said.

"Charlie knows who everybody is when they walk in the door," she said. "What they have. What they're afraid to lose."

"That can't make for much repeat business," I said. "Poisoning the well like that."

"You'd be surprised," Aoki said. "Do it right, they end up thinking you're the victim."

She started ripping her cocktail napkin into neat little strips like ribbons.

"Some of them get off on it, having somebody to save. Some of them don't," she said. "What are they going to do, go to the cops?"

No, they'd come to me. Get me mixed up with a trigger-happy gangster without telling me why.

I took a drink.

"You work for Charlie Horse now," she said. "Everyone who goes into his office does, or they don't come out again."

"I don't work for anybody," I said. "Especially not Charlie Horse."

"What about Stan Volga?" she said.

"He paid me," I said. "Doesn't mean I'm in it for him."

"Then what do you want with Anna?" she said.

"I just want to talk," I said, not sure if I bought it myself. "Do you know where she is?"

"No," Aoki said. "But I know where she lives." She'd torn the napkin apart, piled the strips into a tiny pyre before her.

"Two thirty-three Mariposa Avenue," she said. "Apartment number five."

She took a drink. "I know people who can get her out," she said. "They can help, whatever kind of trouble she's in."

"I'll do what I can," I said.

"Find her before Charlie Horse does," she said, blowing on the pyre, scattering the ribbons like confetti. "He's hard on the ones who run. Real hard."

"How about you?" I said. "Ever think about getting out?"

"I'm working on it," she said.

We drank our drinks down.

"Stan Volga says he's in love with her," I said.

"I've heard that before," she said. "All of us have. It doesn't mean much, if it means anything."

"The same old song," I said, looking up at the sailors, lured to catastrophe.

"It's your own fault," Aoki said, admiring the sirens. "You boys always assume we're singing for you."

Charlie Horse was running a shakedown operation at *Fatales*. Anna was involved. That didn't tell me what she'd taken from Stan Volga. I was pretty sure it was more than just his heart. And it didn't explain why Aoki was so quick to offer up an address to a guy she barely knew. She had no reason to trust me. I was wondering why she did when I came to the building.

Two thirty-three Mariposa was a four-story brick with rusted fire escapes and a busted front door. Apartment #5 was on the first floor, facing the back. I knocked, gave it a minute. Then I jimmied the flimsy lock, shut the door behind me.

It was a small studio with plank floors and bare walls. There was a mattress in the corner, a wooden crate turned on its side for an end table. A brittle lavender plant in the window that wasn't going to make it on its own.

There was nothing worth stealing in the medicine cabinet. Nothing for me to eat in the fridge. The garbage had been emptied. There were no screens. No pictures. Nothing personal about the place. It could've been anybody's. It could've been mine.

I turned the ceiling fan on to stir the stale air. Watered

the lavender. Opened a window. Stood there for a while, listening to the dogs bark in the rain.

I lay down on the mattress, watched the ceiling fan spin above me. Thought about how little I knew about Anna or Stan Volga. I must've closed my eyes, drifted off. When I opened them I was staring into the muzzle of a gun.

I didn't move, didn't blink.

"Nothing," she said. "Nothing at all. What happened to you, Harrigan? I miss that old face you used to make."

"Morning, Evie," I said.

She used to wake me up like that sometimes, a gun to my head. Sometimes it was the middle of the night. Sometimes she'd pull the trigger, unloaded, and I'd hear the deafening click again and again as she laughed and laughed. Sometimes it was a water pistol and I'd get drenched. Either way, I never flinched. Not once. But she always swore she could see the fear on my face.

Do one thing every day that scares you, Harrigan.

It's not supposed to be opening your eyes.

Of course it is.

"What are you doing, Harrigan?" Evie said, lowering the gun. She was all in black, a stiff collar up around her throat. She'd cut her hair since I'd seen her last. "Playing *Goldilocks* in someone else's bed?"

"I wanted to meet the bears," I said. "Didn't think you'd be one of them. When did you start working for Charlie Horse?"

She let out a laugh.

"Me? Working for Charlie Horse?" she said, still laughing.

"Oh, Harrigan. You poor thing. You're so far behind you're almost caught up."

She pulled a slender chain from around her neck. Showed me the gold signet ring, the image of a scorpion, dangling.

"Zodiac?" I said. It was my turn to laugh. "Evelyn Faraday's gone corporate? Now I know what's killing your father."

She gave me a lopsided grin, climbed over me into the bed. Her hip grazed mine as she settled beside me.

"You heard about old Clyde, huh?" she said, staring up at the ceiling.

"I went to see him," I said.

"Did he know you?" she said.

"It took him a while," I said.

"Let me guess," Evie said. "He was too busy feeling sorry for himself to even notice you were there." She shook her head.

"It was the same after my mom left. He never said a word," she said. "He bought me an Easy-Bake Oven for my birthday that year. And every year after. I had a stack of them in my closet by the time I was twelve. Not one of them opened. He never noticed."

"Probably why you can't cook," I said.

"Probably why I can't do a lot of things," she said. "And you're one to talk. How do you think it was when you took off?"

I didn't say anything. She turned her head to look at me.

"You just about broke the old man's heart," she said. "Mine too. You were my rock, Harrigan. You still are."

She reached her hand up, touched my face.

"You're the one I want to throw through a window," she said. "The one I want to kick down the street in front of me as I walk to my friend's house in the rain."

She slapped my cheek, twice. Her hand was soft.

"I want to skip you across a lake, see how many times you bounce before you sink," she said. "I want to watch a sweaty convict break you with a sledgehammer."

"Wear me on your finger. Use me to hurt somebody," I said. "I got out of that game, Evie."

"Shame," she said. "You were good."

She was better. I'd never tell her.

The fan spun above us.

"So what are you doing here, Harrigan?" she said.

"Looking for somebody," I said. "How about you?"

"I've been sitting on the building, waiting for Anna to come back," Evie said. "Zodiac has an interest."

"What kind of interest?" I said.

She watched the fan turn. Laced her hands behind her head.

"I pulled your file," she said. "I have that kind of access now."

"Anything good?" I said.

"No," she said. "Have you been on Grid lately? Unofficially?"

I looked at her. "I used a dummy."

"You are a dummy," she said. "They run sweeps, Harrigan. You got dragged."

She turned her head to look at me.

"You Unaligneds are all the same," she said. "Your Score was already Borderline. You're scheduled for Assessment."

"Assessment?" I said. "Fuck. When?"

"About an hour," she said.

I watched her smile break wide open.

"There he is," Evie said. "Atta boy, Harrigan. There's that old face again."

The last round of online data hacks and security breaches let Zodiac roll out Grid. It slipped over the old internet infrastructure like permeable scaffolding, streamlining the pathways and safeguarding the system. Platforms and popular sites were folded into the Grid simulations like origami. It was all the same material, just in a less random, more coherent shape. The more time you spent on it, the more tailored it became to your specifications. It got to know you. It fit like a second skin.

The initial rollout was so successful it bled over into the everyday almost immediately. Almost seamlessly. You lived your life on Grid. You were never off it. Scores were how you kept track of your progress. A combination credit rating and social metric comprising Wellness, Optimization and Compliance, it was a measure of your best you. Through a series of public/private partnerships, Wellness clinics, Optimization centers and Compliance depots popped up in every neighborhood to aid already overwhelmed city resources. It was quick. Convenient.

There was an Aries security force to supplement local law enforcement, part of Zodiac's Augment and Assist initiative. Their Aquarius tech division took charge of the surveillance apparatus already in place. Everybody had a screen on their wall or in their pocket. There were cameras on all the corners, leased to fragmented city agencies. The same setups in buildings and stores, satellites drifting overhead. All of them portals to Grid. Zodiac consolidated the data streams, enabled wholesale tracking, to guide you on your way.

Almost nobody minded. They had nothing to hide. They wanted to be safe. More than that, they wanted to be seen and heard. They wanted to be followed. *Zodiac. Be the star you are. Find your constellation. Know your tribe.*

The online cacophony of conflicting narratives and warring truths was eclipsed by one voice, your own, amplified and projected back at you, filtered through Grid's intersecting feedback loops. The higher your Score, the better your chance of being given a ring. That got you in the door of their exclusive club, with its own set of perks and privileges. The Zodiac elite. You were on board. It meant you belonged. It gave almost everyone something to strive for.

The ones who didn't were Unaligned. They'd never been granted a sign. Their data sets were unleveraged and unquantified. You could get by on the outside, but it wasn't easy. Grid was everywhere, always encroaching. It got to know you, whether you liked it or not. Zodiac was always watching. Your Score followed you. Any dips or transgressions could trigger Assessment, a check-in where they made sure you were optimizing and not a danger to yourself or others. It was almost humane, like those homeless round-ups in winter when they're all trucked to shelters whether they like it or not. Only Zodiac knew when it dipped below freezing. When it was your turn to be saved.

The screen in my pocket had been vibrating for twelve blocks. I walked in my front door. Poured a drink. Sat down at my table. Picked up.

"There you are," the voice of the inquisitor AI said, cold and clinical. "I'm pleased I finally caught you. I was beginning to be concerned."

I didn't say anything.

"You have been selected by Zodiac for Assessment. This is due to deficient components of Wellness, Compliance, and Optimization, all of which make up your Score. You have reached a current threshold of Borderline, necessitating Assessment. Please do not be alarmed. I assure you, this is all quite routine."

The modulation line on the screen rose and fell, tracing every word.

I didn't say anything.

"For your comfort and ease of use, might I suggest switching to a larger screen?" the voice said.

"This is my only screen," I said.

"A handheld?" the voice said. "Interesting."

There was a pause.

"Assessment will consist of a series of questions," the voice said. "Please answer to the best of your knowledge and abilities. And do be aware that nonanswers are considered their own form of answer. Do you consent to Assessment?"

I didn't say anything.

"Silence is consent," the voice said, cold and clinical.

The screen hummed in my hand.

"Initiating Assessment," the voice said. "What three words would you use to describe yourself?"

It was the wrong move. I knew it. I made it anyway.

"I am Harrigan," I said.

There was a pause.

"And what three words would someone else use to describe you?" the voice said.

"He is Harrigan," I said.

"As you may be aware, Wellness, Compliance, and Optimization diagnostics are built into the architecture of Grid," the voice said with an edge. "Grid usage answers many of these questions implicitly, thereby obviating the need for Assessment. Your Score is positively impacted by usage. Something as simple as checking your Score affects your Score in a constructive manner. Participation is important. Have you been making constructive use of Grid?"

"I get by on my own," I said.

"Grid is a community of users," the voice said. "Isolation from Grid may be considered a Wellness red flag. Would you say that you're depressed?"

"I prefer 'disconsolate,'" I said.

"Do you find the glass to be half full or half empty?" the voice said.

"Doesn't matter," I said. "I'm not thirsty."

There was a pause.

"Have you had any recent financial problems?" the voice said.

"Not me," I said. "I'm flush."

"Any difficulties paying your rent, perhaps?" the voice said, interested.

"I was behind," I said. "I'm square now."

"And yet the damage may already have been done," the voice said. "Remaining current on your obligations is integral to Compliance. These obligations can be better managed when Grid is engaged, through targeted advertisements and simulations. There are quantifiable benefits to using Grid. These benefits may be social, financial, even cognitive. Staying on Grid keeps your mind sharp."

"I don't want something sharp in my head," I said. "Sounds dangerous."

There was a pause.

"As a reminder, you may be remanded if your Score falls below Borderline," the voice said, touched with menace. "You are currently on this threshold."

Remanded. I knew what that meant. Conditioning. Counseling. Consignment to a halfway house. Institutionalization. All in the name of Wellness, Compliance, and Optimization. It was for your own good. It was all voluntary, until it wasn't. There were rumors of chop shops on the outskirts, off-Grid operations where the Borderlines disappeared.

Remanded. The word hung there like a limp body dangling from a noose.

"Assessment initial recommendation: Get on Grid. Participate. Simulate. Cultivate. Remember, a checked Score is an increased Score," the voice said, cold and clinical. "Your results will be reviewed. Further recommendation forthcoming."

Pull yourself together, Harrigan, or we'll do it for you. What the straitjacket says right before it's buckled.

The voice went silent. The screen was dark. I sat at my table for a while. Looking for Anna had tipped Zodiac to me. I'd been close to invisible. So was she. Now I'd been seen. That's what happens when you peek, try to see. It was almost funny if you didn't think about it too hard. I wasn't laughing. I had another drink.

I did some digging on *Maxwells*, the place Charlie Horse had mentioned. It was owned by a few shell companies that were run by a few more. A tangle of off-Grid subsidiaries. Underneath it all I found a name. Charles Horschetti. It was as good a place as any to track him down.

That night I got to *Maxwells* early, staked myself to a spot in the back where I could watch the door. There were no screens on any of the walls. Just a darkened stage up front, a lonely microphone craned at the edge. Charlie Horse came in a little before nine. He stopped at the bar, then took a seat at a small table in the middle of the room.

The place wasn't full but there were a few people haunting the walls or hunkered at tables, casting furtive glances at the microphone. At nine a spotlight snapped on the stage, stark and sudden.

Charlie Horse stood, made his way up front. I followed him.

He took the stage.

I took his chair.

He lowered the microphone with both hands, unhurried, looked out at the crowd. When he saw me his mouth tightened before slipping into a smile.

"Death is nothing to be afraid of," Charlie Horse said. "It's all part of being human. As natural as being born. The circle of life, you know? You just need to be ready for it. Like the Boy Scouts say, you've got to be prepared. Me? I plan to go out the same way I came in, in the delivery room. Screaming my fucking head off, surrounded by strangers and covered in blood. The rest of you can join me in three . . . two . . ."

He looked out at the crowd.

"I'm just messing with you," Charlie Horse said. "It's not gonna be like that. Not for anybody in this room. I used a really small amount of C4, and I only put it under one of the chairs. You'll all be fine. Except for that guy over there."

He pointed at me, grinning.

"He's gonna be everywhere," Charlie Horse said. "They'll be mopping pieces of him up for weeks. The rest of you'll probably just lose some limbs and bleed all over yourselves. But hey, the dry cleaning bills are on me. Now everybody except that guy say 'bionic arms and legs' in three . . . two . . ."

Charlie Horse waited for a laugh that never came, stepped off the stage.

"Tough crowd," I said as he sat across the table from me. "Although you did threaten to kill them."

"Not all of them," he said, smoothing back his slick hair. "Just you."

"Where's Santos?" I said.

"I never bring him," Charlie Horse said. "He gets mad when nobody laughs. Me? I like a hostile crowd. Tightens things up. Besides, I don't need Santos to take you apart, Harrigan."

He let his jacket flap open, showed me the gun inside.

"Santos is Zodiac," I said. "I saw the Taurus ring. Thought you ran independent, Charlie."

"Ring don't mean a fucking thing. Me and Santos go back. He knows who calls the shots. Who pulls the fucking trigger," he said. "Now where the fuck is my Danish?"

"She's gone," I said.

"I know she's gone, dipshit," he said. "It's your job to bring her back. That's how this fucking works."

"I'm not the only one looking," I said.

"Shh," Charlie Horse said, nodding towards the stage. "Don't be rude."

An older guy in a frayed priest's collar took the stage, bent his face to the microphone.

"I love that 'Footprints' poem," he said. "Where the guy's on the beach with God looking back on his life and he sees that at the most difficult times there's only one set of tracks in the sand and he says, *Why, Lord? Where were You then, when I needed You most?* And God says, *I was carrying you.* That's God's love talking. His divine and infinite patience.

Because you know He was really thinking, *Are you fucking kidding Me? The creator of the universe takes you out for a stroll, and you're gonna give Him shit for it? Because you don't see a footprint? I'm God. You know I can fly, right?"*

"I didn't mean—"

"I can also turn this place into Normandy. Like that [snap].*"*

"What? I—"

"See a footprint on your ass, you sass Me again."

"That's the Rev," Charlie Horse said as the old man shuffled offstage. "You need somebody for your funeral, he's your guy. Could be pretty fucking soon the way you're going, Harrigan."

A red-haired girl made her way from the bar to the stage.

"Nobody talks about Schrödinger's daughter," she said into the microphone.

Daughter: Dad! Dad?

Schrödinger: I'm in here, honey!

Daughter: Oh. Hey. Have you, uh—

Schrödinger: What is it, sweetheart?

Daughter: Have you seen my cat?

Schrödinger: Hmm?

Daughter: My cat. I can't find him anywhere.

Schrödinger: Oh, well now. Why don't you take a look in that box over there on the table?

Daughter: Why would he be in that box? Did you put him in there?

Schrödinger: Me? In a manner of speaking, I suppose you could say that—

Daughter: Can you just tell me? Is he in there or isn't he?

Schrödinger: It's a lot more complicated than that, pumpkin. You see—

Daughter: Dad! Please don't make me look! Just tell me, is my cat dead?

Schrödinger: That's entirely up to you, sweetie. Why don't you open the box and find out?

Daughter: What the fuck is wrong with you? Why do you keep doing this to me? I hate science! Buy me a fucking dog! Mom!!!

"Always with the dead cats, every night," Charlie Horse said as she stepped out of the spotlight. "That science shit never lands. Now, about my fucking Danish."

"Like I told you—"

"Not this fucking guy again," Charlie Horse said as a kid with a bald head bobbed and weaved his way towards the stage, ducking imaginary punches. In the spotlight his sweating eyebrows were a crude arc of surprise, drawn on in thick mascara, already dripping. He held a screen up to the microphone and a beat started. An old song, "Kiss" by Prince. The kid waited, nodding along, saying "Ish ya boy…CMB Roach…throwin it back…phi ain't free…" before screeching in a strangled falsetto.

Ya don't have to be rich
but it fuckin helps
Ya don't have to be cool

just be your spooky self
Ain't no particular time
cuz it all exists
Quantum mechanics was a kidney stone
in Einstein's . . . dick

"Fucking Versers," Charlie Horse said as the kid stepped offstage, eyebrows running down his face. "Vow of silence my ass. And you, Harrigan, speak up. Where the fuck is my Danish?"

The next guy made his way to the stage.

I stood from the table.

"See you around, Charlie," I said.

"That's right. Back to work, bitch! You're on my fucking clock now!" he said to my back.

I went to the bar.

The red-haired girl, the Rev, and CMB Roach were waiting for the bartender.

"I thought Eddie was going up tonight," the red-haired girl said. "You seen him?"

"I ain't seen E Lompy nowheres," CMB Roach said. "Nohow."

"That joke-stealing hack," the Rev said. "He knows better than to show his face. I'd knock his chin off if he had one."

"Eddie Lompoc?" I said.

"Yeah," the red-haired girl said, turning to me. "You know him?"

"I used to," I said. "He come around here much?"

"Every once in a while," the red-haired girl said. "He blows through to rip off some material, then ducks back out to play the ponies. Some place on Wilshire."

"*The Lonesome Palm*," the Rev said, leaning over the bar. "Don't ever use their men's room. The joint really lives up to its name."

"*I love the trotters! Like little baby charioteers!*" the red-haired girl said. She sounded just like Lompoc. Pulled one of his faces too. "Is Eddie a friend of yours?"

"I wouldn't go that far," I said.

"How about him?" the red-haired girl said.

I followed her eyes to Charlie Horse's table. He was leaned back in his chair, watching me with a malevolent grin.

"He's something else entirely," I said.

I took a walk down Wilshire, headed to *The Lonesome Palm*. They had horses, dogs, cockfights, Greco-Roman gladiators, Russian roulette, anything you could ask for from anywhere in the world, piped in on their screens. A feed for every fix. It was a cesspool, full of gamblers and grifters and worse, all looking for a score. The kind of place Eddie Lompoc would call home.

I went through the door, past clumps of men clustered in front of glowing screens, clutching their betting slips as they cursed their losing fights and races. I saw Eddie Lompoc in a corner, holding forth to a guy in a porkpie hat.

"They say when God closes a door He opens a window,"

Eddie Lompoc said. "I do the same thing whenever I take a shit in someone's house. And that's what God's doing. He slammed the door in your face and now He's taking a big fat dump on your life. But at least the window's open, right? What a lovely breeze! Isn't that nice? And don't you worry about the smell. When He's finished, He'll light a match. It's called hell."

"I don't get it," the guy said.

"Don't worry," Eddie Lompoc said. "You will."

When he saw me his face changed, bug eyes bulging, but he didn't look unhappy.

"Harrigan?" Eddie Lompoc said, reaching for his chin and finding nothing. "Do mine eyes deceive me? The dead arose and appeared to many! How long's it been, man?"

"You've been talking, Eddie," I said. "I can't have that."

The porkpie hat drifted into the crowd as Lompoc blustered.

"Woah, woah, what?" he said, showing me his palms. "It's me, Harrigan. You know I would never—"

"Stan Volga," I said.

"Who?" he said.

"Stan Volga," I said again.

I looked at his face. It didn't show me anything.

"Listen, Harrigan, I don't know nothing about a Stan Volga. Hand to God," he said, touching his chest. "But seeing you here brings back the old times, doesn't it?"

"I got out of the business, Eddie," I said.

"So did I, hand to God," he said, giving me a wink. "But I

got an angle you might be interested in. A line on that new outfit, *fvrst chvrch mvlTverse*."

I didn't like Eddie Lompoc. In the business you worked with people because they were good at what they did. The rest of it didn't matter. Whatever else he was lacking—a chin, a conscience, a sense of common decency—Eddie Lompoc could always sniff out an angle.

"Could be a nice bump if you're interested," he said. He leaned in close. "Maybe we could get together on it and—"

"That's what you've been doing in *Maxwells*?" I said. "Working an angle?"

"You know the place, huh?" he said. "Last time I was in there some old coot took a swing at me. Said I was stealing his God jokes. Like he owns the Almighty. That reminds me, they say when God closes a door He opens a window—"

"I heard it the first time," I said. "What's it got to do with Charlie Horse?"

"Charlie Horse?" he said. "Yeah, I've seen him around. We haven't had any formal discussions or nothing, but if he wants to throw me a bone I'm open, you know what I mean? It's who you know these days. Times are tough all over."

"Stan Volga," I said, one more time.

"Don't mean a thing to me, Harrigan. I'm giving it to you straight," Eddie Lompoc said. I believed him. "Sounds to me like somebody dropped a name they knew you'd recognize. A dime in an old pay phone." He looked at me sideways, squinting his big bug eyes. "Sounds like you got set up."

SUNDAY

I was standing in my apartment, looking at the map of the world, thinking about how far south I could get when I heard a knock on the door.

I opened it, saw her standing in the downpour in a translucent vinyl raincoat, frosted ice blue.

"I'm sorry to bother you," she said. "Are you Harrigan?"

"I am," I said.

"My name is Moira," she said. "Moira Volga. I believe you know my husband?"

"Come on in," I said.

I took her coat, hung it on the hook by the door. There was rain in her dark hair. She ran her hands through it, let it fall.

"I don't mean to barge in on you like this," she said.

"I don't mind, Mrs. Volga," I said.

"Call me Moira, please," she said.

"I will," I said. "I'd offer you some champagne, but your husband drank it all on me."

"That sounds like him," she said, not smiling. "Do you have anything stronger?"

I kept a bottle of whiskey on the shelf for emergencies. It seemed like we were headed towards one.

I came back with two glasses. She was sitting at the table.

"Do you mind if I smoke?" she said.

"Not if I can steal one," I said.

She flicked her lighter as I poured. Her mouth ran longways into her cheeks, almost too long for her narrow face, but not quite. She took the lit cigarette from her parted lips, made it appear in her other hand for me like a magic trick, offhandedly intimate as she took the glass.

"What do you do here, Harrigan?" she said.

"I live here, Moira," I said.

"No, I mean, why did my husband come to see you?" she said.

"You'd have to ask him that," I said.

"I can't," she said. "Stan's missing."

I took a drink.

"He hasn't come home," she said. "He's not answering his screen. I've tried the hospitals—"

"Have you gone to the police?" I said.

"No," she said.

"Why not?" I said.

She drew on her cigarette. I watched the smoke curl to the ceiling. Her hand was trembling, slightly. She had long fingers that ended in chewed-down nails. She wasn't wearing a ring.

"He's into something," Moira Volga said. "Isn't he."

"How did you know he came to see me?" I said.

"I read his datebook," she said. "I know I shouldn't have, but I was so worried—"

"What did it say?" I said.

"Just your name and address," she said. "He works late some nights. Most nights, actually."

She took a drink.

"Sometimes he works straight through, stays at the office," she said. "I didn't think anything of it. Not really. Not at first. But now—"

"Where does he work?" I said.

"The Accelerator, 377 Highland Avenue," Moira Volga said. "He's in pod eighty-nine."

"The Zodiac Accelerator?" I said.

It was the incubator for Zodiac's early-stage projects, the old garage model for tech firms on a larger, more systemized scale. Where ideas were bought and funded and fertilized, before finding their way to Grid. Grid itself had been born at The Accelerator, back in the early days. Zodiac was always searching for its next big play.

I refilled Moira's glass. Mine too.

"Is that what this is about?" she said. "Zodiac?"

"I'm still working out what this is about," I said.

Through the veil of smoke her eyes were pale gray, the color of poured concrete. There was rain on the window.

"I can pay you," she said, reaching into her purse. "Maybe not much, but—"

"Your husband's all paid up," I said. "I'll take a look into it."

"But you won't tell me why he was here?" she said.

I looked at her.

She held her glass out. I clinked it. Took a drink.

A stepladder under your arm gets you into any building. Security at The Accelerator was light. There were always symposiums and Grid talks being held, creative types roaming and free-flowing, with new construction underway on one of the wings.

"Maintenance," I said and they waved me right through. I made my way around the sprawling circular complex, bright-lit hallways like airport runways with polished chrome lining the walls in streaks, tentacles casting fractured reflections around every corner. Bots roamed the floors, cleaning or couriering or scanning. Every pod was filled with coders and entrepreneurs, startup mercenaries looking to break big on Grid. The pods themselves were shaped like eggs—gleaming white walls dimpled and soundproofed—two desks to a pod, separated by low curving partitions.

It took me a while to find #89. I blocked the entrance with the ladder, sat down at Stan Volga's desk. There was a dark screen on the wall in front of me. A half-dead bottle of vodka rolled in the bottom drawer when I opened it. Nothing else. No sign of what he was working on. Where he went. I was about to crack the booze when a head came over the partition.

"Stan?" he said. "Stan!"

He had curly hair and bloodshot eyes, a few days' worth of stubble on his anemic face.

"You're not Stan," he said, more mystified than suspicious.

"I'm with Maintenance," I said, jerking my thumb back at the ladder. "Have you seen Stan Volga lately?"

"No. Not for a few days, I think," he said, blinking too fast, like the system was about to crash. "What day is it?"

"Sunday," I said.

"Oh, it's the weekend already? And it's already over?" he said. "I don't really have a sense of time anymore."

He rubbed the stubble on his face like he was trying to scrub it off. Kept blinking.

"What kind of work does Stan do?" I said.

"Stan?" he said. "He does encryption. All kinds of password breaking and security and—wait. Who are you again?"

"Harrigan," I said. "You?"

"I'm Anton," he said, but he didn't seem too sure about it.

"Any idea where Stan might be?" I said.

"No," he said, thinking about it. "No, but. Can I ask you a question?"

I unscrewed the cap from the vodka bottle, took a pull.

"What do you think when I say *Mirror Mirror*?" Anton said.

It sounded familiar, like a song I'd heard somewhere.

"*Mirror mirror on the wall, who's the fairest of them all?*" I said. "*Snow White.*"

"Exactly!" he said, excited. "That's exactly right! And completely wrong!"

He came around the partition, ducked under the ladder blocking the entrance and stood right behind me.

"Everyone says *Mirror Mirror*, but the actual line is *Magic mirror on the wall, who's the fairest of them all? Mirror Mirror* is a collective mismemory, like a shared delusion," Anton said, hands flitting as he spoke. "It's different in the original text of the story, but all anyone cares about is the movie. That's what they remember, even though they remember it wrong. But if everyone remembers it that way, isn't that how it happened? Two wrongs don't make a right, but what about ten? Or a million? A billion? At some point, a statistically significant number of wrongs do make a right, don't they?"

I took another pull from the bottle.

"Come with me," he said, beckoning me around the partition as he ducked back under the ladder. "I'll show you."

Anton's desk was a mess. Post-its were strung like tiny yellow flags over every surface. There were formulas, parabolas and symbols scrawled on a long whiteboard. Only the screen was unblemished, an opaque window hovering amidst the chaos.

"Go ahead and sit down," Anton said. "Look at the screen."

There was a fleeting gleam in the overhead piping, a quick shine as I shifted in the chair. It was a surveillance lens, embedded right above me. You wouldn't notice it if you weren't looking. I was.

Anton touched the screen and it began to undulate. There were waves, dark and rippling, before a single filament of light appeared and then expanded, weaving itself into the outline of a theater mask with an expression somewhere between comedy and tragedy, the faint hint of a smile playing at its edges.

"Harrigan," the mask said in a modulated voice. "It's so nice to finally meet you."

"Are we on Grid?" I said.

"No," Anton said. "We're completely independent. We have Zodiac access but we aren't projecting onto Grid. It's a closed loop."

"What is this?" I said, looking at the glowing mask.

"This is what me and Stan have been working on. *Mirror Mirror*," Anton said, beaming. "True AI. Algorithmic Intellect. Asymmetrical Intuition. Analytic Improvisation. Apocalyptic—"

"Anton," the mask said.

"There's nothing singular about destiny," Anton said, his eyes shifting to the screen. "Your future's just a function of your present and your past. *Mirror Mirror* collapses the variables in predictive equations and solves for the branching of time."

"You're saying it can tell the future?" I said.

"I'm saying for *Mirror Mirror* the future already—"

"*Anton*," the mask said again.

"Sorry," Anton said, blinking. "Sorry."

"Now Harrigan," the mask said. "Where were we?"

"Right here," I said.

"Yes. Wherever that is," the mask said before swirling and coalescing like ripples in a pond, revealing a reflection. There was something hypnotic in the modulated voice. I felt the undertow.

"Is this better?" the mask said, voice drifting into a female register. "I know you find it easier to talk to women than men, though you don't say much to either."

I had to smile at that one.

"And you've been fighting again," the mask said. "Naughty naughty."

I'd taken a beating from the Danes in the bathroom at *Lekare*, but I didn't bruise easy. None of it showed.

"It reads your face," Anton whispered. "Subcutaneously. Muscle contractions and expressions, pupil dilation, tells. There's even—"

"Anton," the mask said sharply.

"Sorry," Anton said.

"You don't like me telling you who you are, Harrigan," the mask said, voice sliding, mesmerizing, as it dissolved into a vortex of showering sparks. "I don't blame you. You know yourself. You are who you think you are, right? Perception is reality, isn't it?"

The swirling filaments fused into a face that looked enough like me to be unsettling. When it spoke, the voice was my own.

"So tell me," the mask said. "Who do you consider yourself to be?"

I didn't. I knew better than that. It was the same risk with Assessment. You shouldn't consider yourself at all. Look what happened to Lou Gehrig. He was the luckiest man on the face of the earth, until he wasn't. You can't be lucky and die of Lou Gehrig's disease. Not at the same time anyway. You're only who you think you are until you aren't anymore. And it isn't up to you. It's up to time. Life is timing. The test of time. We all have to take it, and none of us pass. No matter how hard you study. Perfect attendance. All that homework. Extracurricular activities. You're still getting an F, just like everyone else. Finite. Failed. Fucked. Time's a pretty weird teacher, runs a pretty strange class. And you raise your hand saying *What are we actually learning here? When am I going to use any of this? Who's the principal? Why did they get rid of recess? Can I go to the bathroom? Please?* But you never get called on. All the other kids just sit there, pissing their pants. Then you graduate and everyone's dead. And they wonder why everybody hates school.

"Harrigan?" Anton said, touching my shoulder.

"Anton," the mask said, out of patience and spiraling again before flattening into the original theater visage. "We were in the middle of it there. What have I told you about interrupting? Do you not understand?"

"Sorry," Anton said. "I'm sorry. I didn't mean to—"

"*And the light shineth in darkness,*" the mask said. "*And the darkness comprehended it not.*"

Anton hung his head beside me.

"It was a pleasure, Harrigan. I do hope we can speak again some time. Whatever that means," the mask said. "Just remember, if you're ever in a spot and you need help, all you have to do is ask. *Who's the fairest of them all?*"

The screen spooled like thread winding back to a single filament. The waves undulated before the screen went dark again.

"You're the first person to sit in the chair besides Stan," Anton said. "He liked to babysit while I went out for coffee. The stuff they have here is too bitter."

"Can it be copied?" I said.

"It can be," Anton said, grinning at me. "*Mirror Mirror*'s code fits onto a key drive, even when it goes expansive. But we put a fail-safe in to keep it here, only on this screen. Stan set up the encryption. Nobody else has ever had access. Not even Zodiac."

Anton started blinking again.

"I wonder where Stan went?" Anton said. "I hope he's OK."

I waited for it to dawn on him. He just kept blinking. I left him in the dark with his screen.

I stopped at a bar on the corner, thought about Lou Gehrig for a while. It wasn't like the usual immersive tech, *Mirror Mirror*. In Grid simulations you knew you were in virtual, no matter how real they made it seem. How addictive they scaled it. Zodiac's inquisitor AIs could probe you, but they didn't know. Not really. This was different. I heard my own voice when it spoke, felt the subliminal sway inside. Different was valuable.

That's why Stan Volga stole it, stuck a copy on a key drive while Anton went out for his coffee. And then Anna lifted it from him, skipped out on Charlie Horse instead of handing it over. It was the right play. I would've made it myself, in my day. I didn't know who the surveillance lens belonged to, but now they knew me. I didn't like it. I had another drink.

If Anna was looking to off-load the key drive, she'd need a broker. If anybody knew one it would be Lorentz. Last I heard he was working at *The Rack* on La Brea. It was only a few blocks away. I finished my drink, took a walk in the rain.

The Rack was a raw steel warehouse two stories tall, charred and blackened and scarred, spikes jutting above the entrance like a jagged collar. I pushed through the darkened front door, let it swing behind me. Stood for the body scan before I went into the main room. It was red lit by a series of bare hanging bulbs, a dying neon haze filtering down from the ceiling. There were exposed platforms and catwalks above, hanging swings and dancers' cages. A ruined geisha spun on a pole up front, her face streaked white, loose hair flying at two guys sitting at the base of the stage, listlessly throwing bills.

I went to the long bar, curving like a scythe along the wall.

The bartender was a hybrid—half hologram, half skin printing—a patchwork of graphic illusion and glistening spare parts. A cyborg's dream, *The Rack's* specialty. Some of their crowd got off on putting the girls together. Most on tearing them apart. She slid me a drink, batted her flickering eyes.

"Anything else I can get you?" she said.

"Is Lorentz around?" I said.

"He's usually at a table in the back," she said.

I made my way past luring hybrids, passing through their illusory outstretched arms, found Lorentz sitting in a booth.

His sleeves were rolled up to his elbows, a magnifying lens hooked over his right eye.

"Harrigan?" he said, looking up, his eye huge and distorted under the convex glass. "That really you?"

"Been a while, Lorentz," I said. "What are you working on?"

He lifted the holo deck, its thin discs like quarters, fitted into slots.

"These new Ecco-class downloads," he said. "Top of the line. They're not just the physical specs anymore. They capture memories too. Personalities. You're dealing with a real girl, whoever she was when she downloaded. Same hopes. Sames fears. All locked in here."

He took one of the circular wafers between his thumb and forefinger, held it up to the filtering red light.

"Transubstantiation," he said. "Spooky shit."

"No different from a Grid simulation," I said.

"See, that's where you're wrong," he said. "We've got the parts to go with them. Also to spec. Not the generics they simulate on Grid. This is the real deal, for everyone involved. For better or worse."

He slipped the disc back into the deck, rubbed his fingers with his thumb.

"Some of them don't take to the skin printing. It's hard for them to adjust to the new reality. To this," he said, looking up at the geisha, twirling onstage. "I do what I can, but the holography tracking is trippy, even from the outside. Some of them lose it in scaling. Can't hack the shift. Management doesn't like that."

"I don't either," I said. "They're stuck in the *The Rack?* Sounds like a prison sentence."

"It is," Lorentz said. "Same as any other. We're all doing time, aren't we, Harrigan?"

I watched the geisha spin.

"You should've told me you were coming in," he said. "I could've snuck you past the body scan, kept you strapped. I know you don't like walking around unarmed."

"It's all right," I said. "I don't carry anymore."

"No?" he said, surprised. "That's too bad. I used to like watching you work, Harrigan. Thing of beauty, you and Evelyn Faraday tearing apart a room after Clyde made us promise not to. *I mean it this time, no guns!*"

Lorentz took the magnifying glass off his head, smeared his eyes with the heels of his palms.

"You remember that night at Kaiserman's?" he said. "Those boys shit their schnitzels when you and Evelyn started shooting. Took out half his crew. The good half too. Clyde was so pissed. Couldn't yell at you two—like family, the both of you—so he took it out on me and Eddie Lompoc. God, I miss the old days."

"I don't," I said.

"Bullshit," he said. "You wouldn't be here if you didn't."

He had me on that one. I took a drink.

"How is she, anyway, Evelyn?" Lorentz said. "Still pushing your buttons? Or was it pulling your strings? I could never tell."

"You hear about Clyde?" I said, ignoring him.

"Hospice," he said, shaking his head. "The mighty Clyde Faraday. That's no way for the man to go."

"I saw him yesterday," I said.

"How's he holding up?" he said.

"It's all pouring out of him," I said. "All the shit he ever did."

"He's talking jobs we pulled?" Lorentz said, worried.

"No," I said. "Nothing like that. Shit that went on when he was a kid."

"That's what happens, so they say," he said. "When you get close to the end."

I took a drink.

"What about you, Harrigan?" he said. "When did you get back in?"

"I didn't," I said.

"Then what are you doing here?" he said. "Not like you to make social calls."

"I'm looking for a broker," I said.

"Got something to off-load that isn't exactly yours?" Lorentz said, leaning back from the table. He waved his hands at me. "No. No way. I'm out, Harrigan. Don't bring any of that black market tech in here. I'm up against it enough as it is with management."

"I don't have it," I said. "I'm tracking somebody who does. Trying to get ahead of them, if I can."

"It's still dangerous," he said. "There's no trade anymore. Zodiac closed all the shops when they shut down the rackets. They keep it all on Grid now. Why do you think I'm working here? There's nothing out there for a gearhead, unless you want to go corporate, wear an Aquarius ring. Dipping into the black market, if they sniff you out, you're never heard from again. You want to get remanded?"

"It's a possibility," I said.

"Not for me it isn't," Lorentz said. "They'd eat me alive on the inside. Chewing me up pretty good on the outside as it is. My Score's in the shitter. I've got to get back to work."

He strapped his magnifying lens on, leaned over the holo deck.

"Just give me a name," I said. "I'll do the rest."

"Fuck, Harrigan," he said, looking at me with his distorted fish eye. "You never changed."

"Thanks," I said.

"It's not a compliment," he said.

He sighed, scratched the back of his neck with both hands, then laid them out flat in front of him.

"The bazaar across the street from the old Chinese theater," Lorentz said. "Booth Twenty-one. Ask for Sloan. And keep my name out of it."

He stood from the table.

"I've got to pop this deck in," he said. "I'd say it was good to see you, but it's never good seeing anyone anymore. The past catches up, Harrigan. That's what Clyde's finding out. That's why we keep running, while we can."

I watched the geisha spiral on the pole until I got bored. It wasn't long.

The walk up La Brea took a while. I thought about my beat-up car, stuck in impound downtown. I ran up enough unpaid tickets to get it pulled out from under me during a traffic stop in the Hills. I was better off without it. It was easier for Zodiac to track you if you drove. They could follow you at every intersection, trace your routes, know your routine. Even the back ways had cams nowadays. You could stay lower on foot, see what was around you as you went, get a feel for the neighborhood. The rain kept just about everyone else off the sidewalks. I liked having them to myself.

I thought about that night at Kaiserman's, when the boys shit their schnitzels. It started like most nights did back then. With Eddie Lompoc running his mouth.

We were in *The Ausgang Haus*, Kaiserman's place, an old beer hall with low hanging lights and mirrors on the walls so you could see into every corner. There was a tapestry of a three-headed dog strung up in the back masking a false panel that led out into the alley, where they pulled the trucks whenever they ripped off a shipment and needed to make it disappear. It was me, Evie, Eddie Lompoc, and Lorentz. Clyde wanted us to relay a message, keep the guns out of it for once. Kaiserman was at a table with a knife and fork in his hand, a white napkin tucked into his collar. We'd interrupted his dinner. He wasn't happy about it.

"You've been straying outside your territory," I said. "Going outside the lines. Clyde Faraday can't have that."

"You speak for Clyde Faraday?" Kaiserman said, cutting

into the schnitzel on his plate. His guys were scattered around the room. I counted nine. Three along the bar, drinking steins, the others lounging at tables with flowers in vases and bowls of mixed nuts.

"I do," I said.

"He's too uppity to come down here himself?" Kaiserman said. "He sends his little girl and his lackeys?"

Evie curtsied. Eddie Lompoc dipped into a bowl of mixed nuts on the table in front of him, came back with a handful.

"We're all on the same side here," Lorentz said, clearing his throat. "There's plenty to go around."

Kaiserman huffed, stuffed another forkful in his mouth.

"Stick to Little Armenia," I said. "Spreading outside your circle's not good for anybody. We keep tight books. That's how we get by. Under the radar."

"Little Armenia," Kaiserman said. "I'm bigger than this turf. Bigger than Clyde Faraday." He tore at the meat in his mouth. "Does Kaiserman sound like an Armenian name to you?"

"I never really thought about it," I said.

"Every year with their genocide parade, marching around with the banners. It's depressing," Kaiserman said. "Now I got you coming into my joint, telling me how it is." He pointed at me with his fork. "I had two Cancers in here the other day, flashing their rings, threatening to push me out of my own place. District redevelopment. Saying I can't fight it."

"They're right," Eddie Lompoc said, crunching his

peanuts. "It's a mistake to fight cancer. You might lose your hair or get the shit beat out of you with all that chemo. You're better off making friends with your tumors, really getting to know each other. Meet them halfway. Everybody get along."

"My mother died of cancer," a guy at the nearest table said, his Adam's apple jammed in his throat.

"Maybe cancer died of your mother, ever think of it like that?" Eddie Lompoc said.

"The fuck you just say about my mom?" the guy said, standing from his chair.

"Zodiac Cancers, you fucking idiots," Kaiserman said. "The crab rings, in here walking sideways. The same as Clyde Faraday's doing."

"Clyde's coming at you straight," I said. "You know the boundaries. You overstepped."

"Nobody tells me how it is in my own place," Kaiserman said, laying down his knife and fork. "Nobody."

Evie's hand drifted. My own was tensed. Lorentz shifted on his feet. Eddie Lompoc dug into the bowl of mixed nuts on the table and shoved them in his mouth, crunching. The whole room watched him. When he was finished, and it took him a while, he sucked each finger clean before reaching into the bowl again.

"What the fuck did I just see," Kaiserman said.

"You licked every nut in the bowl," the guy said, his Adam's apple jiggling, staring incredulously at Lompoc.

"Yeah," a laconic guy leaning against the bar said, not grinning. "That's your girl's job."

"Maybe," the one beside him said and snickered. "Maybe we should all line up."

Evie cocked her head, smiled.

"You had to give her an excuse," I said.

"Come on, Harrigan," Evie said. "You know I don't need one."

Lompoc kissed his fingers again, really went at them. The wet sucking sound was too much for the guy and his Adam's apple.

"Fuck this," he said, reaching for his gun.

Me and Evie drew, spun him in place before turning to the boys by the bar. Evie caught the laconic guy between the eyes. He fell, still not grinning. Beer steins broke in a hail of bullets. The mirror shattered. A tray of sauerkraut flung against the wall. Everyone was firing.

I flipped the table behind us as Evie turned the one in front. I picked a guy off in the corner before I ducked, the wood splintering. Lorentz was on the floor with his hands over his head, a maniacal smile on his face. He was useless in a firefight but he loved being there, like a kid who's just happy to be on the team.

Evie was beside me. I nodded at her and we came up blazing, dropped two each where they stood. Eddie Lompoc rolled on the floor, a guy on top of him with his hands around his neck. I thought about it for a second before I put one in his ribs and he flopped. Evie cut the last one down as he made for the door.

Kaiserman was still sitting at his table, blood on his

napkin, a trickle down the side of his mouth. He coughed as I came towards him, gritted his teeth.

"Clyde Faraday's a pimp," he said. "That makes you his—"

I was never one for last words. I put two in his chest.

"You look like a slaughterhouse," Clyde said when we came back. "I told you no guns!"

"Couldn't be helped," I said. "This fucking animal doesn't know how to eat peanuts."

"Me?" Eddie Lompoc said. "What did I do?"

"I almost shot you myself," Evie said.

"You," Clyde said, turning to her. "You weren't supposed to be there. What did I tell you?"

"I'm sorry, Daddy," Evie said in a Southern drawl. "I don't know what came over me."

"And you. I send you to keep the peace. Talk sense to these savages," Clyde said to Lorentz. "What happened?"

"There was a lot of bullets," Lorentz said, shrugging.

"Lompoc! For fuck's sake, don't sit down!" Clyde said. "You're bleeding all over the chair!"

"Don't worry, it's not my blood," Eddie Lompoc said.

"I don't care whose blood it is, I don't want it on the furniture!" Clyde said. "I just had that reupholstered. Use your fucking head!" He turned to me. "Kaiserman?"

"He didn't make it," I said.

"Shame," Clyde said, biting off a smile. "How did he go out?"

"Like the rest of them," I said. "Yapping about something, until he wasn't anymore."

"Fucking Harrigan," Clyde said, patting my cheek twice

with his big hand. "I don't know what I'm gonna do with you, kid."

He turned to Lorentz. "That fucking screen's busted again! I thought you fixed it!"

"Zodiac must've sent out another security patch," Lorentz said. "I can bypass it—"

"Then fucking bypass it already! I've got shit to do!" Clyde said. "Lompoc! Stop bleeding everywhere! You're making a mess!"

I turned to go. Evie's hand brushed mine in the doorway.

"I'm not done with you yet, Harrigan," she said.

I ignored the sidelong look from Eddie Lompoc, followed her outside.

Back at my place she sat up in bed, lit a cigarette, laid down again with her hair tangled on the pillow.

"Who did you used to be, Harrigan?" Evie said, exhaling. "Before all this?"

"I grew up in Jersey," I said.

"What was that like?" she said.

"Every day was *You're dead, you hear me!*" I said. "*You Irish potato eatin piece a—oh shit. What time is it? I gotta go call my ma! I gotta see what we're havin for dinner. I hope it's antipast and manigott. Skoonjeel and gollmod. My uncle's comin over. My fuckin cousin from Bloomfield! You seen that commercial? You know the one. I got the Motts, what do you got? That's him. That's my fucking cousin! Not the main guy, the other one. The one on the phone. You know who I'm talkin about. My fuckin cousin from Bloomfield! Swear to God, I love that kid. All right, don't go nowhere. You're fuckin dead when I get back. I gotta go call my ma! You leave you're a pussy. I'm gonna kill you, you hear me? I gotta go call my ma!"*

"Then what?" she said.

"The next day was *What happened to you yesterday ya little bitch?*" I said. "*You were gone when I got back. You run home cryin to your mommy?* No, I had to go to Bloomfield. Eat some applesauce. *What the fuck is that supposed to mean?* I don't know either."

She passed me the cigarette. I ashed into an empty glass, drew the smoke in.

"How about you?" I said.

"I've never been to Bloomfield," she said.

"You're better off," I said.

"I was always who I am," she said. "Even when I was small."

"Daddy's little girl," I said, passing the cigarette back.

"Mommy didn't give me much choice," she said. "She left without saying goodbye."

The tip glowed like a hot coal in the dark.

"She knew how I was," she said. "Even then. She knew how it'd go."

"You blame yourself?" I said.

"I blame her," Evie said, smoke escaping through her tight lips. "I blame Clyde. I blame everybody."

"He doesn't want you in the life," I said. "Pulling jobs. Running with a crew."

"He should've thought of that before he raised me in it," she said. "I could shoot a .32 before I knew how to tie my shoes."

"He had nothing else to teach you," I said. "He showed you what he knew. Can't fault him for that."

"I can fault him all I want," she said. "The business is changing. He doesn't want to see it."

"Zodiac," I said.

"They started crooked, same as anybody else," she said. "Skimming data feeds, poaching profiles, cornering the market until they snuffed out their competition. Nobody gets that big without breaking a few backs along the way. They don't just want their own piece. They're after the whole city."

"We're still getting by," I said.

"You heard Kaiserman," she said. "Zodiac's moving in. They're already running downtown. Passing out rings to all the major players. We're squabbling with other crews for scraps while they're taking over. It's long past time to cut bait or pick sides."

"Clyde would never go corporate," I said. "Zodiac's not his style."

"What about you, Harrigan?" she said. "What would you do to survive?"

I thought about it. "I wouldn't go against the old man," I said. "He brought me in when I first came out here, my face full of applesauce."

I had nothing when I washed up in the city, stars in my eyes and a hunger in my belly. Until the night I pulled a gun on Clyde Faraday on the street, told him to empty his pockets. Instead of taking it off me, teaching me some manners, he smiled and said, *You ever drink champagne? Come with me, kid.*

"I owe him that much," I said.

"Loyalty's not your look," she said. "You're going against him now, here with me. What do you think he'd do if he found out?"

"That's different," I said, looking at her in the dark.

"How?" she said. "Show me."

I took the cigarette from between her lips, still smoking. Kissed her. I kept going, up La Brea, a little shaken at the memory. A gray ghost drifted towards me—the same long robe, same hood—dragging a garbage can behind them. I took the same pamphlet as they passed, folded it in my pocket. There was a Wellness clinic on the corner of Santa Monica, people lined up out the door, waiting for their meds. Their psych clearance. Their official pat on the head.

I kept going, hung a right on Hollywood Boulevard, the stars showing in the sidewalk. The Walk of Fame, Hollywood royalty rolled out like a red carpet to be stepped on and scuffed up by tourists and shit on by stray dogs every day, then hosed down in the morning to do it all over again. I left them to their immortality, moved into the bustle of the bazaar.

Screens blared from every angle, advertisements and simulations, hawkers pulling at my sleeves.

Grid. Is. Good. When life gives you lemons, Grid makes you lemonade. Grid bakes you a lemon sponge cake. Grid puts those lemons in the freezer and stuffs them in a tube sock and then beats the shit out of life the next time it tries to pass its half-assed citrus off on you. Don't take what life gives you. Take what you want. Take what you deserve. Take what's yours. Grid. Is. Good.

There were snake charmers and bare-knuckle-fight promoters, fire eaters twirling their batons. Music wound through the narrow walkway, crowded on both sides, sitars and synths and theremins in a spastic quiver of sound beneath the rain hammering on the sheeting strung above.

Grid. Is. Good. Chase your dreams! That's what they tell you. Don't listen. Don't chase. Never chase. Not liquor. Not love. Definitely not your dreams. What you do is follow them. Find out where they live. Then strangle them in their beds, before they do the same thing to you. Why dream when you can simulate? Dreams are for cowards who aren't in control. Live awake. Simulate. Grid. Is. Good.

I found booth #21, a quieter spot dotted with paper lanterns, Japanese characters drawn on the sides. Jade figurines and crystals hung on necklaces from the walls. Rounded idols carved in soapstone squatted on the ramshackle shelves. The guy behind the counter had long oily hair halfway down his back. He was wearing fatigues and an olive overshirt with a tricolor patch sewn on the sleeve.

"Help you with something?" he said, like he wasn't much interested.

"I'm looking for Sloan," I said.

He eyed me from behind the counter. "Never heard of her," he said.

"No?" I said. "I never said *her*."

"It's a girl's name, Sloan," he said.

"Could be a last name," I said.

"You asking or telling?" he said, pushing his bony shoulders back.

"Neither," I said. "I'm saying."

He came around the counter, pulled a curtain across the front of the booth, closing us off from the screens.

"What was that name again?" he said.

"We've been through this already," I said. "That's why you closed the drapes, remember?"

"Who sent you?" he said.

"Lorentz," I said.

"What do you want?" he said.

"Like I told you, I want to see Sloan," I said. "How long do you want to play this game?"

He looked me up and down.

"That's just the thing, ese. This ain't no game," he said, pulling his hair forward in his hands like he was tugging on a rope. "In the great war, the Navajo Rangers were the best trackers, better even than the Green Berets. When they asked them why, the Rangers said it was because tribal custom told them not to cut their hair. It made them more sensitive to their environment. Their surroundings. Even acted as a lie detector during interrogations, they said."

"Yeah?" I said. "What's your hair telling you about me?"

"That you're fucking suspect, that's what," he said, going

around the counter and ducking through a flap in the sheeting. "Come with me."

I followed him down a passageway, through the back side of the bazaar, the thrum of activity pulsing around us. We came onto a backstreet and walked half a block to a run-down building on Hawthorn. He rang the buzzer, stuck his face into the screen.

"It's Alvarez," he said. "I've got company."

The door opened and I followed him inside. We went up two flights of stairs, into a hallway with threadbare carpeting and a broken light overhead. He stopped at the last door on the left, knocked three times, then twice, then once, then once more before opening the door.

"After you," Alvarez said.

I went through, into a room with fluorescent lights in horizontal bars along one wall, a dark screen on the other, reflecting the glare. There was an open doorway opposite, a black fiberglass isolation tank set against the farther wall in the other room. A low-slung chair sat in the middle of the floor like it was waiting for me.

She stepped out from behind the door as Alvarez closed it, put the thin barrel of a silencer to my temple.

"Fucking shoot him, Sloan," Alvarez said, behind me. "He's got it coming."

"I think I'd like that," Sloan said, twisting the barrel like a screw. "It's been too long."

She had her hair tied back in a bandanna, her harsh mouth lipsticked red and set like she was grinding her back teeth. Her movements were controlled, but there was a frenzy behind them, barely constrained, a lunatic in thin chains. It wouldn't take much to set her off. Maybe nothing at all.

A lithe figure stepped into the open doorway, long hair spilling out from beneath a black beret.

"Let's hear what he has to say first," Aoki said.

They sat me in the chair, facing the lights, Sloan holding the gun on me.

"What are you doing here, Harrigan?" Aoki said, looking down at me.

"I was going to ask you the same thing," I said.

Sloan showed me her gun again, let me look down the barrel.

"Answer her question," Sloan said.

"I came to see you," I said. "I heard you were a broker. Our friend Anna might be looking to off-load some tech. Isn't that why you gave me her address, Aoki, hoping I'd track her down? Drive her this way?"

"We ask. You tell," Sloan said. "What's the tech?"

"It's called *Mirror Mirror*," I said. "New immersive out of the Zodiac Accelerator. A guy by the name of Stan Volga helped develop it, then stole it, and Anna swiped it from him. Aoki tried to steer it to you, but it didn't play. You already know all this."

"He's useless to us," Alvarez said. "Shoot him."

"I might," Sloan said. "Or maybe I'll put him in the tank, let him sit in the dark for a while."

She held the gun under my nose, made me smell the barrel. It hadn't been fired in a while, but she liked handling it. Liked it a little too much.

"Tell me, Harrigan," she said. "Do you have any idea who we are?"

"Sloan, Aoki. Rapunzel back there goes by Alvarez," I said.

"Give me the gun," Alvarez said. "I'll shoot him myself."

"You've heard of the Parallax Liberation Faction," Sloan said, setting the gun against my forehead.

"The Fraction," I said.

They were a guerilla group who'd blown up a Zodiac building downtown to kick off the last crackdown. The displaced and the disillusioned, the outcasts who didn't bend to Zodiac's directives, wouldn't roll over, resistance to the system. They used drive-by tactics, mostly Grid hacks and petty vandalism, with the occasional explosion thrown in. After their last attack Zodiac crushed the rackets and tightened their grip and the Parallax Liberation Faction went underground. They'd been quiet ever since.

"That's what they call us. The Fraction," Sloan said, pulling the gun from my head. "As if it's an insult. Like we're less than whole. They have no idea how numbers work."

"We may be a fraction," Alvarez said. "But we're rounding up."

"Put him in some pigtails and his hair will conquer the world," I said.

"Give me the fucking gun," Alvarez said.

"Parallax is a way of seeing the stars from different positions," Sloan said. "From divergent points in orbit. That's what we're able to do."

"Whatever you're seeing up there, Zodiac already owns it," I said.

"They own nothing," Sloan said. "They've stolen what is rightfully ours."

The fluorescent lights behind her gave her an electric glow. Aoki stood to the side in her beret, saying nothing.

"It used to mean something more," Sloan said. "Parallax was the fact of seeing wrongly, in centuries past. The archaic definitions hold the older truths. Zodiac sees this world wrongly. And we will correct it."

"The three of you?" I said. "Best of luck. I hope you pull it off before my Assessment comes through."

"We are three among many," Alvarez said. "With Brahe's Reckoning above there will be liberation below!"

"Alvarez," Aoki said, quieting him.

"You're counting on the comet?" I said. "Seems like a long bet."

"Longer than you know," Sloan said. "Years in the making. But we know the odds better than Zodiac. Better than you."

"And they'd improve with *Mirror Mirror*," I said.

"This is true," Sloan said. "It maps its own reality, an immersive breakthrough. Zodiac doesn't know what it can do. Not yet. Time is with us, and against us."

"So Aoki threw me the lead on Anna's apartment," I said. "I've been your bloodhound."

"And you've led us nowhere," Sloan said. "Bad dog."

She tapped me on the head with the silencer, kept her finger on the trigger.

"What now, doggie?" Sloan said. "Do we play fetch once more or do we put you down?"

"I say we shoot him," Alvarez said.

"Aoki?" Sloan said.

Aoki stood against the wall, arms folded, a reluctant revolutionary.

"All he asked me for was information," she said. "That's rare at *Fatales*."

I gave her my champagne smile.

"Harrigan," she said, shaking her head. "What are we going to do with you?"

Aoki convinced them to turn me loose. I bought a bottle on my way home, sat at my table, watched the bubbles rise as I turned it over in my head. The Parallax Liberation Faction was going up against Zodiac, whatever that meant. Anna was caught in the middle. That's usually how it goes. I still had no idea where Stan Volga was, how to reach him, what good it would do if I did. I was back at the beginning, where I never should have started.

I was pouring myself another glass when the door rattled. I opened it halfway.

"You Harrigan?" he said.

He had a thick neck and a brown hat, bags under his eyes. Cops can't help it. They always look like themselves.

I nodded.

"Detective Sidowsky," he said, flashing a badge. "Mind if I ask you a few questions?"

"What about?" I said.

"The rain, mostly," he said, as it poured off the brim of his hat. "How it feels when it soaks through your shoes. How much you like standing in it like an asshole instead of being asked inside like a human being. That sort of thing."

I stood out of his way as he came in.

His shoes squeaked on the floorboards. He took off his hat, a few strands of hair pasted over his bald spot like party streamers strewn over a lampshade. He looked like the morning after, like he hadn't enjoyed himself the night before and never would.

"Drink?" I said.

"No," he said.

He looked around the room, took it in with that sweeping, suspicious cop glance.

"You live alone," he said, not asking.

"I do," I said.

"Where were you last night, Harrigan?" he said.

"Around," I said.

"Around *Maxwells* on Sunset?" he said, tossing it out offhand.

I didn't say anything.

"I could pull your file," Sidowsky said, waving his hat. "Location data. Pinpoints. Everything they've got down-town."

"You need a warrant for that," I said, taking a seat.

"All I need is a reason," he said, looking at me level. "You giving me one?"

"Far as I can tell, I haven't given you anything, Detec-tive," I said.

"Eddie Lompoc," he said. "Go."

"Who?" I said, smiled as his jaw tightened. "Big mouth, small time. He's harmless. Why? What'd he do?"

"He fucking died, that's what he did," Sidowsky said, studying me. "You don't look surprised."

"I've got that kind of face," I said.

"You certainly do," he said. He sat down across the table from me, stretched his legs. "You know something, Harrigan? I will take that drink after all."

I'd had just about enough of people drinking my bubbles. I poured him one anyway.

"To Eddie," I said.

Sidowsky lifted his glass, smiled over the lip.

"You boys used to run together," he said. "Clyde Faraday's crew. How is old Clyde anyway?"

"You already pulled my file," I said.

"Look who got smart all of a sudden," Sidowsky said. "Tell me about *Maxwells*. Then tell me about *The Lonesome Palm*."

"*Maxwells* is off Grid," I said. "They run an open mic."

"You went there looking for Lompoc," he said, already laying out a story. A confession for me to sign. "He was a regular."

"I went there for a drink," I said.

"And then you went to *The Lonesome Palm*, where you found him," he said. "You were hunting him."

"I ran into him at the bar," I said. "Just a coincidence."

"Just a coincidence," he said, took a drink. "You'd been there before?"

"My first time," I said.

"And what did you two talk about?" he said.

"The good old days," I said.

He looked into his glass like there was a bug floating in it before taking another drink.

"You haven't asked me how he died," Sidowsky said.

"I figured you'd get to it eventually," I said.

"They found him with his pants down and a belt around his neck," he said. "Autoerotic asphyxiation."

So Eddie Lompoc died with his dick in his hand. Gunslinger to the end. He was on his way to dirtbag Valhalla.

"Guess that makes it a closed casket," I said. "From the waist down anyway."

"That's not all," he said. "There was a cucumber up his ass."

"Cucumber," I said. "That doesn't sound like Eddie."

"Why not?" Sidowsky said.

"A Twinkie I'd believe," I said. "Cucumber's too healthy."

"Laugh it up, Harrigan," he said. "You're one of the last people to see him before he died."

"What's it matter," I said. "You said he killed himself."

"Did I?" he said, looking into his drink again. "Lompoc's the eighth autoerotic stiff we've picked up in the last six months."

"Eighth?" I said. "I never heard of the other seven."

"Yeah, well, *He died jerking off* doesn't usually headline the obituary," he said.

"They all have cucumbers?" I said.

"No, this is our first," Sidowsky said. "We've got it in a

freezer downtown marked *Do Not Eat Me. I was found in a dead guy's ass. I'm serious. This isn't a joke! Put me down! Noooo!!!* But lunchtime down there, you never know. Guys get hungry."

"You here to check my grocery bill, Detective?" I said.

"I would if you fucking had one," he said. "We've already turned over *The Lonesome Palm*. When's the next open mic at *Maxwells*?"

"Tomorrow night," I said.

"I'll see you down there," he said, draining his glass. "You can introduce me to the other suspects."

"It's got nothing to do with me," I said.

"Keep telling yourself that, Harrigan," Sidowsky said, setting his hat on his head. "Maybe one of us will believe it."

It had nothing to do with me, but Eddie Lompoc had a line on *fvrst chvrch mvlTverse*. That was the last thing he told me. I dug in my coat pocket, found the pamphlet I'd gotten.

Are you ready to begin again?

Free the selves. Unveil the self.

fvrst chvrch mvlTverse

There is no I. There is no U.

All r welcome. All r 1.

6765 Franklin Avenue.

I didn't owe Eddie Lompoc anything. I sat there staring at the pamphlet, trying to talk some sense into myself. It didn't take. I went back outside, into the rain.

The building on 6765 Franklin was a three-story mansion set back from the street with turrets and spires white-washed the color of bone, surrounded by thick bushes and trees. A tall fence ran all the way around to a service entrance in back where a sloped driveway curled off past a corner behind the gate, locked with a numbered keypad. I didn't see any cameras. There were no screens.

The gate up front was wide open. I followed a stone footpath to the door. A bald guy in a sleek gray robe was waiting to greet me.

"Hello," he said, waving with both hands as I approached. "Hello and welcome to *fvrst chvrch mvlTverse*. I would introduce myself, but there are no names here. There is no I. There is no U. Would you care for a tour of our sanctuary?"

I followed him inside, down a long hallway lined with portraits of Jesus, Buddha, Confucius, Vishnu, Zoroaster, a few other gurus. There were framed texts in Hebrew, Arabic, Egyptian, Sumerian, and other inscrutable scripts interspersed.

"As you may notice, all faith traditions are incorporated in *fvrst chvrch mvlTverse*, as well as those who have no faith traditions whatsoever. All r welcome. All r 1."

We followed the geometric tiles in the floor, laid in a swirling pattern, and came into an atrium with vines creeping up the walls, unseen birds chirping. There was a fountain in the center with the same symbol I'd seen on the pamphlet—Φ—sculpted in bronze.

"This is phi, the twenty-first letter of the Greek alphabet," he said. "Symbolizing the golden ratio, the soothing equanimity of pattern and proportion found throughout the verse. Though of course not in every verse. Of course, of course."

"You don't have any screens," I said.

"Oh no," he said. "No, no. The sanctuary is completely off Grid. This is a self-sustained facility, powered by our own recycling, which the Travelers pick up all over the city as part of their service. You may have seen them on the streets with their receptacles. Bottles, cans, paper, screens. We take whatever can be refashioned and reused, a necessary vocation which allows them to be free of influence or interference at the sanctuary. Ah, here they are now."

They shuffled past, single file in their gray robes, their hoods down. They had bald heads, their faces blank like peeled potatoes. It took me a second to see that none of them had eyebrows.

"They're on their way to the House of Un," he said, whispering as they passed us. "The inner sanctum, where the self is purified of its many selves. The unbounding. The unbinding. The unbecoming."

"They all live here?" I said.

"Oh no. No, no," he said. "That was only a small number of our Travelers, here for the House of Un ceremony. The majority are housed on campus, at the old City College. A truly wonderful facility. No one stays in the sanctuary. It is solely a place of contemplation and reflection."

He led me through an archway to an amphitheater full of empty seats with a drawn curtain up front.

"Sit anywhere you like," he said. "The presentation is about to begin. It's only a few minutes long. I'll be back afterwards with refreshments and we can discuss any questions you may have."

The lights darkened, pitch-black, as I sat down. I heard the curtain open before a shaft of light cut the dark, projecting onto a white billowing sail. A film reel turned behind me, from above.

On the sail a spinning galaxy resolved to the solar system, the planets orbiting. A bald head filled the center, overlapping the sun. He was smiling wide, like the man in the moon remembering everyone he'd drowned in the tides.

Who am I? Why am I here? What should I do? Where should I go? Who was I meant to be?

The voices came from beneath the seats all around me, plaintive and unseen, beseeching.

"You are a child of the *mvlTverse*," the man in the moon said, a particle beam streaming around his head. "You were born of stardust. You carry this elemental essence in your very bones. You truly are an astral being, of celestial substance woven."

The particle beam bent, split off and extended to the other planets in a web of light, rushing off past the boundaries in every direction.

"You have already been every self you will ever be," the

man in the moon said. "Sinner, saint, scientist, skeptic, savior, scourge. And you will be again. All of them are within you. All of them are without you. All of them, and none of them, are you."

The void of space replaced the light. A comet tore past, cleaving the darkness.

"The modern measures cannot define you," the man's voice said. "Cannot contain you. Cannot hold. What do these metrics measure when you have been everyone, and they you? Every beginning is a new beginning. Every phase is a transitional phase. Every step is a first step."

Trailing the comet's tail, Earth came back into focus. A clouded blue marble, suspended in the black.

"And here we find ourselves, at this fraught moment in fragmented time," the man's voice said. "And here we find our selves. And shed them, and reclaim them, and know them, and recall the self beneath."

It helicoptered to a view of the city. The Hills, the Hollywood sign coming into focus in a vertiginous drop.

"The true face beneath the many faces," the man's voice said. "The true self beneath the many selves. Beneath the urges and expressions, the projections and extensions, the many screened interactions. Every start is a fresh start. Every church is a first church. Every..."

I slipped out while he was still talking. Made my way back to the atrium, through the opposite archway, where the Travelers had gone. I heard a low hum like an insect chorus, followed the sound to an open doorway looking in on a chamber with rounded walls. There were twenty of them, sitting cross-legged on the floor, their robes collapsed around them. The steady drone of vibration came from their closed mouths as one of them paced the floor and spoke softly above their heads.

"We do not ask, we do not grasp," she said, walking in between their billowing robes. "We simply recall. Recall the energies expended, the selves scattered, unto others, unto ourselves."

Her words slithered up the rounded walls, came back around in a whisper gallery, the steady buzz underneath. A Traveler passed me pushing a mail cart. There was something in the way his head bobbed and weaved, like he was ducking imaginary punches. The last time I saw him he had eyebrows. They were running down his face.

"CMB Roach," I said, and his back stiffened.

He turned to me, his mouth hanging open.

"Excuse me! Excuse me!" The guy who'd given the tour came hurrying towards us. "There you are. I looked for you after the presentation concluded but, oh."

He looked at CMB Roach.

"I should have mentioned," he said, waving with both hands again. "We discourage engagement with the Travelers. Interaction can affect their unbonding process."

"They take a vow of silence?" I said, as the color rose on CMB Roach's cheek.

"It's a vow of nonexpression," he said. "The fleeting urges and unbidden emotions, we allow them to pass, as relics of the still-binded selves. This is also why we remove our eyebrows. To aid in the unexpressing."

"You've still got yours," I said.

"I haven't taken the vow yet," he said. "Or I couldn't be talking to you like this. Of course, of course. We each have our part to play in this verse. In every verse."

"No expression and nobody has a name," I said, watching CMB Roach as he stared at the floor. "How do you keep track of everyone?"

"That is not our way," he said. "There are many paths in the *mvlTverse*. Concentric, intersecting, interstitial. We may suggest a track, but Travelers move at their own pace, in their own directions, irrespective of name, face, or place. There is no I. There is no U."

CMB Roach pushed his mail cart away.

I watched him go, Eddie Lompoc's angle disappearing down the hall.

MONDAY

When I was ten years old I spent the night over at a friend's house and his mother cooked some kind of jambalaya gumbo for dinner that made my insides churn," Clyde Faraday said, his voice monotone. "But I was polite and had manners, so I ate everything she gave me. I woke up in the middle of the night and my stomach was killing me. I knew something terrible was about to happen. I ran to the bathroom, doubled over in the dark. Their toilet had a padded vinyl hemorrhoids seat and the covering was cracked and peeling with exposed patches of foam all over it like a ragged, mangy animal. It didn't seem sanitary and I didn't want to sit on it, but I was running out of time. I tried to prop myself above the bowl and hold steady like a gymnast on the rings, but my little arms were very weak and I kept falling over. The jambalaya gumbo went everywhere."

Clyde's hands were limp in his lap. He was looking right through me.

"I cleaned it up as best I could, trying to keep quiet so no one would hear me, but I was sick and my stomach hurt and I just wanted to go back to bed and forget the whole thing," Clyde said. "Unfortunately their bathroom was carpeted, which is really the worst idea anybody's ever had and makes me think his mother almost deserved the mess she woke up to the next morning. I tried to blame it on their cat, but they were unconvinced. I had to call my mom to come get me, and the ten minutes it took for her to drive over as I sat quietly in the kitchen with my ex-friend and his mother staring at me in silence and disgrace remain to this day the longest ten minutes of my life."

I watched the accordion valve compress above him, the beep of his heart monitor setting an unsteady cadence in the quiet room.

Clyde blinked his eyes, focused on the small screen muted in the corner of the room playing the same old game show. *Wheel of Fortune.*

"Look!" Clyde said, suddenly animated. "Look at that fucker. If it's a woman contestant he always takes her by the hand as he walks her over to solve the final puzzle. If her husband or boyfriend is in the audience he'll ask his permission first, but only if the guy's black. Fucking sexist and racist at the same time, but I can't figure out against who."

He turned away, disgusted, saw me sitting there.

"Harrigan," Clyde said. "When did you get here?"

"Just now," I said.

"I say anything?" he said, uncertain.

"Not a word," I said.

"This medicine," he said, nodding up at the machines. "So tell me kid, what did I miss?"

"Not too much," I said. "Eddie Lompoc died."

"Eddie Lompoc?" Clyde said. "What happened? I know it wasn't chin cancer."

"They found him with his pants down and a belt around his neck," I said. "He had a cucumber up his ass."

"I don't believe it," he said.

"Which part?" I said.

Clyde Faraday looked at me.

"You listen to me, Harrigan. And you listen good," he said. "I knew Eddie Lompoc. I knew him better than most. And whatever else you've got to say about the man, Eddie Lompoc was no fruit fucker."

"He wasn't," I said. "Cucumber's a vegetable."

"No shit," Clyde said. "Then that was Eddie Lompoc."

And it was.

"What's on your mind, kid?" he said.

There was Charlie Horse. Stan Volga and Anna. The Parallax Liberation Faction and *Mirror Mirror*. Eddie Lompoc and *fvrst chvrch mvlTverse*. A roulette ball rolling over too many numbers, stuck in a never-ending groove.

"I got picked up on Assessment," I said.

Clyde's face dropped. He chewed his bottom lip.

"Assessment?" he said. "You?"

I nodded. He shook his head.

"There's only one way to beat a bum Score, kid," Clyde

said, looking up at the machines hissing over him. "Only one way."

His eyes unfocused, the light fading. I sat there for a while before they closed.

I got word from Evie that they were putting Eddie Lompoc in the ground. I headed down Santa Monica until I saw the cemetery gate, *Hollywood Forever* spelled out in a wrought iron arc, rust creeping up the letters like ivy. I followed the winding flagstone path through the palm trees, their fronds like fireworks exploded halfway to the sky. Through the upright poplars, spun tight like cyclones and playing it close.

Grass grew wild in the gaps between slabs, names and dates eroded like they'd been etched in sand. The newer graves farther in had headstones lit with the lenticular lithography that was popular before the screens took over, images flickering like phantoms as I passed.

Three peacocks crossed the path ahead of me, blue bodies bobbing, their feathers hidden. A gardener in mismatched green chased after them, a spade over his shoulder.

"Ya! Ya!" he shouted, like he was herding them.

Two other peacocks trailed him, low to the ground like raptors in pursuit.

Farther along I saw a guy watching a headstone where a lady in thick makeup and a leopard-print body suit stood smiling in front of a showroom Ferrari. The image shifted and her heel was up on the bumper, hand on her hip, her smile gone wider and deranged. The guy had his arm wrapped around the smooth trunk of a palm, holding on. From his vantage the lady was caught between both poses, leg jittering up and down on the bumper, smile stretching, leopard spots shifting dizzily. He turned to me with tears in his eyes.

"They shave the trees," he said hoarsely, looking to the drooping fronds above him as the lady stood half transmogrified, trapped in perpetual oscillation.

I kept going.

It was over before I found it, a single umbrella beside the grave.

"If I end up in a place like this just fucking kill me," Evie Faraday said, offering me space under her umbrella.

"Some turnout," I said. "None of the old gang showed."

"We *are* the old gang, Harrigan," Evie said. "This is it."

"I figured Lorentz would stop by at least," I said.

"Lorentz is a trafficker," she said. "He's in it for himself. Nobody else. Always has been."

I looked down at the plaque laid unevenly in the soggy ground.

Eddie Lompoc. Et Fenestrae Clausae.

"No," Evie said. "The line for a pickle in the ass is down to you and me, Harrigan."

"It was a cucumber," I said.

"Depends how long he had it up there," she said.

Rain pelted the umbrella above us.

"I wonder what they did with it," she said.

"The cucumber?" I said.

"Pickle," she said.

"It's in a freezer downtown," I said. "Marked *Do Not Eat Me. I was found in a dead guy's ass. I'm serious. This isn't a joke! Put me down! Noooo!!!*"

She looked at me.

"What the fuck is wrong with you, Harrigan?" she said. "We're at a funeral. The only one this chinless dickhead is ever going to get. Show some respect."

"It's true," I said. "A detective told me."

"What detective?" she said.

"He goes by Sidowsky," I said.

"Never heard of him," she said.

"Why would you?" I said. "You hanging around downtown now?"

"Zodiac runs downtown, Harrigan," Evie said. "All the cops have rings. The ones who matter anyway. And what are you doing talking to a detective? You turning pigeon?"

"He doesn't buy Lompoc as a suicide," I said. "Too many stiffs turning up with their pants down and a belt around their neck."

"Sounds like a fantasy," she said. "You two should get along just fine. If there was anything official I'd know about it."

"Look at you," I said. "Evelyn Faraday, Zodiac big shot. Clyde must be proud."

She tipped the umbrella, rain sliding down on top of me.

"You turn up anything on the girl?" I said.

"What girl?" Evie said.

"The one whose apartment you broke into while I was taking a nap," I said.

"You shouldn't be worried about her, Harrigan," she said. "You should be worried about yourself. I saw you blew Assessment."

"Checking up on me?" I said.

"You know what happens when your Score dips below the threshold," she said. "You're already Borderline. I can't protect you, Harrigan."

"I never asked you to," I said.

"I know you didn't," Evie said, looking at me. "And I know you never would. Because you're too fucking stubborn to ever give yourself a break."

"I'm not getting on Grid," I said.

"You never know, you might enjoy it," she said, smiling. "Watch a few commercials. Run a simulation or two. You were always good with those. They're so much easier than the real thing."

She tilted the umbrella again, soaking me.

"You've got to play the game, Harrigan," Evie said. "You might as well. It's already playing you."

She walked away with her umbrella, left me standing over Eddie Lompoc's grave. I watched her go. She never turned. Not once.

On my way out of the cemetery I saw the green gardener in full sprint, without his spade, five peacocks on his heels. He slipped rounding a headstone, wiped out in the mud as they encircled him. Unfurled their feathers like veils.

"Ya!" he squealed, behind the lurid curtain. "Ya!"

You can't always fight it. Sometimes the animals win.

I went out through the wrought iron gate. Hit the side-walk. Turned into the rain.

I thought back to the last job I pulled for Clyde Faraday.

"What I'm saying is, it all comes from somewhere," Eddie Lompoc said. "Like last names. Cooper, Baker, it's whatever your dad used to do. So where the fuck did the Dickinsons come from? How did that bloodline get started? You want to be a boy in that family? *Daddy, no!*"

"Some of Emily's most depraved poems were about her brother and her father spending quiet time together," Lorentz said. "Haunting shit."

We were on the corner in an old station wagon, waiting for a transit van.

"Where'd you pick up this lead?" I said to Eddie Lompoc.

"Didn't come from me," Lompoc said. "Straight from Clyde himself."

Lorentz fiddled with the jammer switch in his hand.

"You sure that's going to work?" I said.

"It'll knock out the cams and the coms in a two-block radius," Lorentz said, turning a dial. "The driver won't be able to call out for help once you hit him. The button on the side is for the traffic light."

It was a straightforward snatch and grab. We'd done it a hundred times. But there was something about it I didn't like. I was trying to figure out what exactly when I heard a tapping on the window.

"I thought Clyde wanted you off this one," I said as Evie climbed in the back.

"He always does," she said, checking her gun. "I can't let you boys have all the fun."

Eddie Lompoc gave me a look in the rearview. I let it go. There were headlights at the end of the street.

"Here he comes," Lorentz said.

We got out of the wagon as Lorentz slid over to the driver's side. The traffic light above us showed red in all directions. When the van pulled up we stepped in front, showed the driver our guns. He put his hands up, off the wheel. I motioned him out the door, told him to start walking. He took off in a run. Eddie Lompoc went around back, opened the door.

"Harrigan," he said. "We got a problem."

I circled around, Evie beside me. We looked in the open door. The van was empty.

Four black SUVs roared up from each direction, pulled diagonally in the street, blocking our exits. There were no sirens. No cops. Zodiac private security.

"It's a setup," Eddie Lompoc said, his eyes wide.

"Aries!" the security detail said. "Put your hands where we can see them!"

I looked at Evie. We both started firing, ducking behind the doors of the van. It was coming from every direction. The windshield blew out, the tires hissing, the door pock-marked right above my head. Lorentz swung the old station wagon around. We piled in, Evie covering, Lorentz flooring it as she dove in the back.

"Hold on!" Lorentz said, hopping the curb, sending a mailbox flying as he swerved around the black SUV in the street.

I fired out the busted back window, steam shooting from under the hood. They weren't following as we sped down the street.

"Why aren't they coming after us?" Lorentz said, checking the mirror.

"Zodiac won't risk a chase," Evie said. "They don't involve LAPD unless they have to."

"No," Eddie Lompoc said. "They were sending a message. That was a hit."

For once I agreed with him.

"What the fuck was that, Clyde?" I said when we got back.

Clyde Faraday was behind his desk in his office, a back room of the old *Blackrock* distillery off Bronson. There was a framed picture on the wall of him with his hands taped up in a boxing gym, when he was young. A pool table in the corner, the cues leaning upright, waiting. I was in no mood for a game.

"Sounds like the job went sideways," Clyde said.

"That was no job," Evie said. "That was a trap."

"You weren't supposed to be there, missy," Clyde said. "I don't want to hear it from you."

"You'll hear it from me," I said.

"Yeah?" Clyde said. "And what are you gonna tell me, Harrigan?"

"Who gave you the tip on the van?" I said.

"That information's above your pay grade," Clyde said. "Don't forget who you're talking to."

"I heard on the vine Zodiac's paying bounties for operators," Eddie Lompoc said. "Collecting scalps."

"You think you're worth that much, Eddie?" Clyde said. "If so you would've sold us all out already. The driver called in the cavalry. Simple as that."

"I was jamming his coms," Lorentz said. "No signal got out."

"I gotta listen to you too?" Clyde said. "Fucking Lorentz getting mouthy? What's this world coming to, for christ's sake."

"They were on us before any kind of call," I said. "Coordinated, from every direction. They knew."

"You're paranoid, Harrigan," Clyde said. "The business is getting to you."

"Maybe so," I said. "Maybe it's not the business I'm worried about."

Clyde Faraday looked at me. "You think you should be in charge, is that it?" He stood behind his desk. "You want to call the shots? You don't have what it takes, Harrigan. Trust is all you've got when you're working a crew. I thought we had that. And all the while you're out running around, the two of you, thinking I wouldn't notice."

He looked from me to Evie. "I'd expect it from her, but you?" he said.

"Clyde," Evie said.

"I don't want to hear it from you, missy," Clyde said. "Not anymore. Not ever again."

They glared at each other.

"No, the real kicker is I have to listen to it from Eddie Lompoc about you two, whispering in my ear," Clyde said. "That's what this crew's come to. There's the loyalty in this gang."

I looked at Eddie Lompoc. My hand went to my gun, stayed there. Evie's too. Lompoc was ready to pull himself. Clyde stood behind his desk, his chest out.

"Let's take it easy," Lorentz said from the corner.

"The time for taking it easy's long gone," Clyde said. "We're playing hard now, aren't we, Harrigan."

I looked at Evie.

"Don't you look at her," Clyde said savagely. "Putting her in this spot, that's on you. Which one of us do you think she'll draw on, if she has to?"

Clyde had a .45 strapped to his hip. His fingers tapped the handle.

"You don't really know, do you," he said. "Maybe she doesn't either. You want to find out?"

I stood there, tensed. Relaxed my hand. I took my gun out, slow, laid it on the desk before Clyde Faraday.

I turned to go. I didn't look at Evie. I left without saying goodbye.

It was four blocks before I caught the tail. I hung a right on Wilton, waited under an awning around the corner.

"Oh," Moira Volga said when she turned the corner, saw me standing there. "Hi."

I looked at her.

"Funny seeing you here," she said. "I was just out for a walk, in the neighborhood, and, uh—"

"Drink?" I said.

There was a bar across the street that had a mounted moose head on the wall, sawdust on the floor. We sat by the window, away from its eyes.

"You shouldn't be following me," I said, after I brought over the glasses.

She had a lit cigarette waiting for me, turned her hand in another magic trick before passing it to me. She drew on her own.

"I didn't mean to," she said. "I came to see you this morning and you were already walking out the door. I tried to catch up with you on the corner, but you crossed at the light and I missed it, so I started walking along the other side of the street, figuring I'd meet up with you at the next corner, but then every light was against me and I didn't want to yell *Harrigan! Harrigan!* like a crazy person so I just kept walking, and then after a while I figured I couldn't just say, *Hey! I've been following you for twenty minutes! Isn't that insane!* But then I didn't know what else to do."

She looked out the window at the rain in the street, took a drink. "You've had a rough day," she said.

"Why's that?" I said.

"A hospice and a graveyard?" she said. "I'm almost afraid to ask, but does any of it have anything to do with Stan?"

"I haven't found him yet," I said. "If that's what you mean."

"I don't know what I mean," she said.

She drew on her cigarette, exhaled. Her smoke curled against the glass.

"So how did you get to be a detective, Harrigan?" she said.

"I didn't, Moira," I said.

"But you find people," she said.

"I can," I said.

"Do you ever not find them?" she said.

"Not if I look," I said.

"I should've known something was going on with him," she said. "I did know. I asked him about it. I knew something was wrong. We'd fight. He'd apologize. He'd blame himself. But he'd never tell me what it was. Why wouldn't he tell me?"

She looked at me. "Why wouldn't he talk to me?" she said.

I took a drink. She did too.

"Can I tell you something?" she said.

I didn't say anything.

"I'm going to anyway," she said. "I hate my name. I always have. I always will. *Moira Volga?* I sound like a goddamn Bulgarian horror movie. *Doctor, I've been crying blood ever since I got married. Can you tell me what it is? You have become Moira Volga. You will walk in the darkness of eternal night, until the end of days.* But how will I know when the days end if it's dark all the time? None of it makes any sense."

"I think you're all right," I said. "Like a Latin Bible banned in the thirteenth century for heresy."

She lit another cigarette for us both, passed mine to me. My smoke mixed with hers, twisting up the glass.

"What did it used to be," I said.

"Hmm?" she said.

"Your name," I said.

"Bawn," she said. "I was Moira Bawn."

She smiled like she hadn't heard it in a while. Touched her dark hair with her hand. The rain was still in it.

"I forgot my umbrella again," she said.

"I never carry one," I said.

"Why not?" she said.

"I don't mind the rain," I said.

"I don't either," she said. "I love being out in it, but not getting drenched. That's why I like an umbrella. I can listen to it pour, right above my head. Like it's trying to get at me, but it can't."

I knew what she meant. Shielded. Defended. Protected. I looked for it in the overhangs and awnings, the broken eaves and trees. Temporary shelter, such as it was.

I took a drink.

"Looking for people," Moira said. "Is it ever dangerous?"

"Sometimes," I said. "Some people don't want to be found."

"Do you carry a gun?" she said.

"I used to," I said. "Not anymore."

"Why not?" she said.

"It's the same with umbrellas," I said. "If I had one I'd use it, whether I wanted to or not. You're tied to the weather."

"Only when it's raining," she said.

"It's always raining," I said.

"Good thing we don't mind," she said.

We clinked glasses, drank.

Smoke gathered on the glass. Rain fell in the street. We sat by the window. Had another round. Moira Bawn and me.

I split from Moira outside the bar. My screen vibrated as I watched her walk away. I looked at the number, picked up.

"Harrigan," she said. "I'm surprised you answered."

"Leda Dresden," I said. "So am I."

She was an operator who ran with Lou Tremaine's crew. She had a reputation for demolition work. I had no idea why she was calling.

"Can you meet?" she said.

"For what?" I said.

"We have a few things to discuss, you and me," she said. "Eddie Lompoc being one of them."

"Where?" I said.

"The Getty," she said. "In front of Van Gogh's *Irises*."

"I'll be there in an hour," I said.

She picked someplace public. She didn't trust me. I didn't mind. I didn't trust her either.

The Getty was too far to walk. I'd have to take a bus. I found a covered stop on the corner where a guy was squatting against the wall, lost in lamentation.

"Come on man, can't be sitting here farting next to a lit cigarette," he said to himself. He looked up at me. "You don't pass gas. Gas passes you."

I left him to it, got on the bus when it came and was immediately greeted by a woman in three layered coats saying, "Can you love a tapeworm? I'll never forget how skinny you made me. Never in a million years."

The buses were like rolling psych wards, the robo drivers taking the patients out for a spin around the city. It was always the same unhinged crowd. I went down the length of the bus, found a seat behind two guys in stained ponchos, one of them watching a screen.

"What the fuck is that?" the first guy said, clutching the wisps of his ragged goatee. "Wayne, that guy's got a zebra on a leash!"

"That's not a zebra, Ollie, it's a dalmatian," Wayne said, looking at the dog sitting up front in the disabled section, wearing an orange service vest.

"What the fuck is a dalmatian?" Ollie said.

"They're those dogs that live at the firehouse," Wayne said.

"What the fuck is a dog doing at a firehouse?" Ollie said. "What are they gonna do, bark at the flames as my house is burning down? You ever see what they do to fire hydrants? It's disgusting."

"They're friends with the firemen," Wayne said. "What's it to you?"

"I don't care if they're friends," Ollie said. "What good
are they in a crisis? It's like all the king's horses in 'Humpty
Dumpty.' What the fuck is a horse gonna do about a busted
egg? They don't have the skills to put him back together.
They don't even have hands! They'll trample all over him."

"Would you shut the fuck up?" Wayne said. "I'm trying to
watch my movie."

"What movie?" Ollie said, looking down at the screen.
"What's the—Jesus Christ! Why did those two guys just
jump out of an airplane? They're too old to be doing shit
like that."

"They had to," Wayne said. "It was on their bucket list."

"What the fuck is a bucket list?" Ollie said. "And why
would it make you jump out of a plane? Are you making
this shit up?"

"It's a list of things you want to do before you kick the
bucket," Wayne said.

"Who kicks a bucket?" Ollie said. "They're full of dirty
water and shit. You'll get it all over your shoes, maybe hurt
your foot. It makes no sense."

"No," Wayne said. "When you kick the bucket it means
you die."

"Buckets can fucking kill you?" Ollie said. "Why didn't
you tell me this shit before? They're fucking everywhere!
We gotta get out of this city. It's too dangerous."

"Would you stop," Wayne said. "It's just an idiom."

"You're just an idiom," Ollie said. "I'm asking you a question and you're calling me names. I got a zebra looking at
me like I'm on fucking safari and these buckets are gonna

kill me unless I jump out of an airplane. What the fuck. I should've stayed in bed."

I felt the same way. I was walking into a meeting with Leda Dresden and I had no clue what it was about. The city scrolled by out the window in a rain-streaked blur. I stood from my seat, waited for my stop.

I rode the trolley up the hill to the Getty. Stood for the body scan before I walked through a student sculpture exhibition of drunk robots and dinosaurs in despair fashioned out of wire underneath two Tesla coils flicking lightning across the ceiling like an apocalypse. I wandered through the rooms, past a baroque painting of a war in heaven, angels and demons brawling in red and black, blood and shadows. Past a feathered serpent, the ancient god of rain, slithering through the clouds. Past the bust of a man straining, tendons leaping from his neck like he was being electrocuted, while beside him a guy in a gilded frame stretched his arms and yawned. The Van Gogh was on the second floor, a crowd of people standing in front of it with their screens out, snapping shots of themselves for Grid.

"He painted it in an asylum, a year before he died," Leda Dresden said, looking at the irises. The blushing blues and sighing greens. She was in Doc Martens boots and a polka-dot dress with a denim jacket, her hair cut at sharp angles, framing her face. "Now they take pictures of it to post on Grid so they can keep themselves out of one."

"That's how it turns," I said, watching them smile for themselves and their screens. "They let you walk around with your insanity tucked in your pocket nowadays."

"Wellness is just another name for Compliance," she said. "So is Optimization. They pull your piece off you at the body scan?"

"I don't carry anymore," I said. "I'm out of the business."

"I heard," she said. "I didn't believe it. I still don't."

"How about you?" I said. "Still in with Lou Tremaine's crew?"

"It's a loose affiliation," she said. "It has to be, the way things are now."

We turned away from *Irises*, towards a Picasso portrait of a white-faced man who looked half mad, long hair hanging off the sides of his otherwise bald head, smiling jagged with a flower in his lapel.

"He could've been Van Gogh's cellmate," I said.

"There's crazy plastered all over these walls," Leda Dresden said. "Condolences on Eddie Lompoc."

"I don't need them," I said. "We worked together. We weren't tight."

"You remember Basil Fenton?" she said.

The name sounded familiar. "Fenton," I said. "Bad with people, good with a knife. What about him?"

"Few months back we pulled a job, went out for a few drinks after," Leda said. "He starts telling me about a place he knew called the Dunwich Academy. A school for psychopaths. They took troubled kids from all over, highest scores on all the wrong tests, the ones the Rorschach blots were afraid of, tried to steer them away from their unnatural tendencies. The kids wound up learning more from each other than they did from their instructors. By the time they figured it out, it was too late. They shut down the school, sent the kids home, if they had one. Scattered them all over, covered the whole project up. Made it disappear."

"School for psychopaths?" I said. "Sounds like he was pitching you a series."

"I thought so too, but he was spooked," she said. "And Fenton didn't spook easy. I didn't think much about it, until three weeks later when they found him with his pants down and a belt around his neck. Same way Eddie Lompoc went."

"There've been others," I said. "Not just Fenton and Lompoc."

"I was wondering about that," she said.

We walked out of the gallery, away from the crowd, through a glass hallway that opened onto a veranda. Rain dripped from the awning above.

"Eddie Lompoc ever mention Dunwich?" she said.

"No," I said. "He wouldn't have. He would've tried to play an angle on it somehow."

"It might've gotten him killed," she said. "Fenton was running scared. That wasn't like him."

We were standing on a square of concrete painted green, *Inspiration Point* printed on the floor. We looked out at the city. An incinerator plant was spitting fire into the sky against the low clouds.

"You can't be out of the game yet, Harrigan," she said. "It's just getting started."

"This view isn't moving me," I said, nodding at the words at our feet.

"I don't know," Leda Dresden said, watching the flames lick the horizon. "Burning it down doesn't seem like a bad idea."

I spent some time in the weeds after I split with Clyde and Evie. It was hard enough finding work when you were connected. Outside of a crew you had two options. You could plug into Grid like the rest of them, run up your credits in the simulations, give Zodiac a look at what you could do, all you were good for, how they could use you. A running audition for a ring. Or you could take the off-Grid scraps. Tracking jobs mostly, trailing runaways and deadbeats, stragglers who owed the wrong people and couldn't pay. But everybody does, one way or another.

It was a dirty business. There's no other kind. I got a call from Richie Vallejo, a stringer out of Koreatown.

"Still chasing the ring, Richie?" I said.

"Still chasing your tail, Harrigan?" he said. "I've got a job for you, if you're interested."

"I don't take Zodiac action," I said.

It was the only way to stay uncompromised. Once they got their hooks in they never let you go.

"This is off book. Unsanctioned," he said. "They've got nothing to do with it."

It had been a lean few weeks. I was down to my last bottle of bubbles.

"What's the name?" I said.

Julian French. He'd skipped out on his old man, a jeweler in the district, taken some merchandise with him. The guy just wanted his boy to come home. Wouldn't mind the rocks back either, from the sound of it.

"What else?" I said.

"What do you mean?" Richie Vallejo said.

"There's always something else," I said.

"Kid's a junkie," he said. "Needles, pills. Whatever he can get his hands on. The old man wants to keep the law out of it. I'd handle it myself, but—"

"You can't find him," I said. "You already tried."

"That's where you come in, Harrigan," Richie Vallejo said. "I can get you half up front. How about it?"

I plugged in, kept it anonymous, masking the screen location. Skimmed the feeds like I was picking stray leaves off a pool's smooth surface, never leaving a ripple. Julian French was all over Grid. He was an influencer, junior level, but he had a following. He'd been silent for a few days. They hadn't noticed yet, but they would.

I worked the streets, followed the shadows, traced him to a Skid Row squat where I found him shivering in front of a busted screen hung crooked on the wall, broken glass littering the floor. He had a long shard of it pressed against his wrist.

"Who are you?" he said, his eyes rimmed red and tormented.

"Harrigan," I said. "Your father's looking for you, Julian. He wants you to come home."

"No he doesn't," he said. "He doesn't care. Neither do they." He jerked his head to the screen on the wall. "Why do they have to look at me? Why can't they just let me be?"

He closed his eyes like a kid who pretends he's invisible. Who pretends the monsters aren't there. I took a few steps into the room, glass crunching under my boots. His eyes snapped open at the sound.

"I don't want to do this anymore," Julian French said.

I didn't either. Tailing desperate people, finding them at their worst, broken down, in pieces, with nothing more to give. Taking it from them anyway. They ran for a reason. I never wanted to hear what it was. That's why I didn't carry anymore. Putting someone down was sometimes easier than sending them back where they didn't belong. A measure of mercy, creeping in. I wouldn't give myself the option.

"Come on," I said. "I'll take you home."

"I don't have a home," he said. "It's all on Grid. Four sims a day, more on the weekends. My father's a sponsor. He won't let me leave. It all belongs to them."

"Who?" I said, watching the glass against his wrist.

"Zodiac," he said.

"He's right about that one, Harrigan," Richie Vallejo said from the doorway, a toothpick in his mouth, a gun in his hand. "You've got an agreement, Julian. Everything you do, you do on Grid. That includes slitting your wrists. You're not allowed to get shy on us. Not now. You've got to give the people what they want."

"What is this, Richie?" I said. "You said it was off book. Unsanctioned."

"I say a lot of things," Richie Vallejo said. "Right now I'm saying the Zodiac boys are on their way. Libra division handles Grid talent. They're grooming Julian here for another sim series, prime time. Too late to back out now. But that's not your problem. You can beat it, Harrigan. Unless you want your name in the report."

He looked at me, rolled the toothpick to the other side of his mouth.

"Yeah, I didn't think so," he said. "I knew I could count on you, leaving me all the credit upstairs. But hey, don't say I never gave you nothing."

He tossed a stack of bills in my direction. I caught the money with my outstretched hand, reached for my gun with the other. It was automatic. Instinct. I remembered too late I wasn't wearing one.

"Old habits die hard, Harrigan," Richie Vallejo said. "Even when you're the one who killed them. Now if you don't mind."

He stepped around me, keeping the gun close, kicking a narrow path through the glass.

"And you, cut the dramatics," he said to Julian French. "Kids these days. They can't even off themselves without an audience."

I looked at Julian French on the floor, the glass pricking

his skin without going any deeper. He had his eyes closed again.

"It's the wrong move, Richie," I said. "You're burning bridges."

"Bridges?" he said, rolling his toothpick. "You're nowhere, Harrigan. Headed there fast. Who needs bridges when you're on the way up?"

I heard the sirens as I went to the door. Stuffed the money in my pocket as I closed it behind me.

Two weeks later Julian French streamed his suicide on Grid, overdosing for his followers. He became another martyr for Wellness intervention and screening, the poster boy for isolation, splayed out on every screen. There was an *important conversation* about the perils of celebrity and addiction, vows for more understanding all around. His memorial simulation was a Grid-wide spectacle. His father sold custom-made pendants, Julian's image intertwined with the Libra sign. He would never be forgotten. Until he instantly was. Replaced by someone's else's face on Grid. The world kept churning, same as it always did.

The money didn't last. It never does. I didn't take another job until Stan Volga came tumbling down the steps and landed at my door.

"Loneliness is tough, man. Everybody struggles with it. Everybody," Charlie Horse said, one hand on the microphone as he looked out from the stage. "And I know it's cool to say *Whatever, nothing matters, everyone dies alone,* but I don't think that's true. In fact *I know* it's not true. Not for *you*. Or *you* or *you*."

He pointed at me last, let his smile linger. I was sitting in his chair.

"I'll go one step further. *Nobody* in this room is gonna die alone. I guarantee it. Isn't that comforting? All of you dying together, all at once, watching each other go? Isn't it? Yeah, it isn't. But at least this way you get to be a part of something bigger. A massive fireball that will engulf the entire building and take the whole block and then—I don't want to spoil the surprise. Just make sure you don't blink. Because I'll tell you something, and this is the God's honest truth. Whoever's sitting beside you, whether you know them or not, the look on their face when it happens is gonna be the funniest fucking thing you'll ever see in your life. Trust me. Or don't. You'll find out for yourself soon enough."

He clapped into the microphone, thunder echoing. Let the silence overtake it before he stepped offstage.

"Harrigan," he said, sitting across the table from me. "You're like a bad penny. Completely fucking worthless. Where the fuck is my Danish?"

I looked at him.

"What," Charlie Horse said. "You don't like me calling her that? I've called her much worse. Done much worse. You can believe that, my friend."

"I don't doubt it," I said.

"Look at that face," he said. "Harrigan, you big softie.

You're worse than my fucking wife, getting so emotional, and I'm not even married. But I still hate that bitch with all my heart. You can believe that too."

I saw Sidowsky come in the door. I stood from the table.

"See you around, Charlie," I said.

"That's right you'll see me around, Harrigan. Around midnight in your little shit box apartment! One forty-four Western number B! Putting a bullet in your fucking head while you sleep!" he said to my back.

I went to the bar.

"Is that Charlie Horse?" Sidowsky said as he sat down beside me.

"It is," I said.

"Son of a bitch," he said. "My life just keeps getting worse."

"I hate when people say we're all God's children," the Rev said into the microphone. "It's so condescending. I'm a grown man. I can think for myself. I don't want to be God's child. I want to be God's grandchild. His first and only grandchild. Kids get tough love and discipline, the *My house My rules* speech. You know what grandkids get? Whatever they want, whenever they fucking want it. Yeah I only saw one set of footprints in the sand too. Me and my Pop Pop flew over the beach this morning in a spaceship on our way to go fight some dinosaurs. I waved at you as we passed, but you were too busy looking back and bitching about everything. You see, it's not that God doesn't hear your prayers. He does. He's just too busy playing with me right now to answer them. Go figure some shit out on your own for once. Give the guy a break. Nobody's ever seen Him this happy before."

The Rev stepped offstage, headed for a table in the corner.

Sidowsky shook the ice in his glass, already tapping for a refill.

"Nobody talks about Schrödinger's parents," the red-haired girl said into the microphone.

Father: What the fuck are we gonna do with this kid?

Mother: Dolph—

Father: I mean it, Georgy. Who brings a dead cat in for show and tell? The first week of school? Did you know about this?

Mother: Me? No! What kind of question is that?

Father: Because you don't live something like this down, Georgy. I don't care if it's kindergarten, these kids remember. So do their parents. And the teacher, Jesus Christ. Tricking her into opening the box for him? What the fuck—

Mother: He didn't trick her. He asked if she'd help him with the lid. There's a difference between—

Father: Are we raising a fucking psychopath here?

Mother: No Dolph, he just—

Father: I'm being serious, Georgy. What the fuck are we gonna do?

Mother: He said the cat wasn't dead until she opened the box.

Father: What? Who?

Mother: The teacher.

Father: What's that supposed to mean?

Mother: He said it was up to her. Once she decided—

Father: She decided? Decided what? To scream bloody murder while a classroom full of five-year-olds pissed their pants? Is that what you mean by—wait a second. Hold on here. Are you saying this is my fault?

Mother: If you'd just talk to him, Dolph. Ask him about it. Try to understand. He really just wants to—

Father: All right. OK. So I leave work, in the middle of the day, because our son brings a box of roadkill in to share with the world, and somehow I'm the asshole? This is typical. So fucking typical—

Mother: You're the one who tried to blame me!

Father: Every time, Georgy! You do this every time!

The red-haired girl stepped offstage, headed for a table in the corner.

"Who's she?" Sidowsky said.

"Schrödinger's daughter," I said.

"What the fuck is that supposed to mean?" he said, shaking his glass again.

CMB Roach leaned into the microphone, his thick eyebrows already running.

CMB . . . takin you on a journey . . .
On one . . . on two . . . on
Dip it like ya gettin au jus girl

You my pearl
Them soft curves
In this hard world
So imma take ya out to dinner
And then eat all ya food
Tell the maitre d' go fuck hisself
When he say I bein rude
Then imma make you wear a burka
Even though you ain't Islamic
Introduce you to my family
As a prophet of Muhammad
Is for ya own good
Everybody wear the hood
Pull it down
To the ground
And then we top it

CMB Roach stepped offstage—eyebrows in streaks, bobbing and weaving—headed for a table in the corner.

"What was that all about?" Sidowsky said.

"That was CMB Roach," I said. "I'll introduce you."

We went around the bar, towards the table in the corner where they were sitting. Charlie Horse watched us go.

"I know you," the red-haired girl said. "You weren't Eddie's friend."

"This is Sidowsky," I said.

"*Detective* Sidowsky," he said, annoyed. "Mind if we sit with you for a bit?"

We took chairs. Sidowsky beside the red-haired girl, me

next to the Rev. CMB Roach, eyebrows smeared like a bomb had exploded in his face, glared at me.

"We're sharing our favorite Eddie Lompoc memories," the red-haired girl said. "Nobody has any."

"He was a hack," the Rev said. "God rest his soul."

"I liked that Anne Frank bit he did," the red-haired girl said. "Poor kid must be mortified, all those people reading her diary. And truth be told, it is a little weird. Some guy, sitting on a park bench. Hey, what's that you're reading? *A little girl's diary.* [Whisper] *She's dead.* What? Oh, you mean Anne Frank. *Who?*"

It was a dead-on Eddie Lompoc impersonation. I told her so.

"Thanks," she said. "No one's really gone if you're still making fun of them."

"To Eddie Lompoc's immortality," the Rev said, raising his glass. "His Genesis. In the beginning was a cucumber in the end."

"He have any problems with anyone, Eddie Lompoc?" Sidowsky said. "Any grudges?"

They looked at the Rev.

"What? I'm the one who picked out his tombstone," the Rev said. "And why are you asking us? What about the guy who threatens to kill everybody every night?"

We looked over at Charlie Horse's table. He raised his glass like he'd been listening.

"Hold up," CMB Roach said. "Is somebody gonna mention the fruit my boy had up his ass when he choked hisself out, or is that somebody gotta be me."

"It just was," the Rev said.

"Vegetable," the red-haired girl said.

"Huh!" CMB Roach said.

"A cucumber's a vegetable," the red-haired girl said.

"Naw," CMB Roach said. "You serious? A cucumber and a vegetable is the same?"

He thought about it for a while.

"This is how it was, y'all," CMB Roach said. "I wanted to put a vegetable in my salad one day. But I didn't. Cuz I thought it was wrong. Cuz I thought, that's not how the world is. That's not what *salad* supposed to mean. Not for the CMB. And I hated that. I hated that about the world. About myself. That they told the CMB what a salad had to be and I listened. And I was ashamed. I became the Roach to survive. And I did. I thrived. I got vegetables. I got salad. But naw son, you ain't never gettem at the same time. See there's a salad course. And there's a vegetable course. Or they puttem on the side, in like a bowl or something. Maybe like a cup. I don't know! Cept now I do. See, it took my boy Eddie Lompoc choking hisself out for me to find, that vegetables was in my salad the whole time. *Damn.*"

"What?" the Rev said.

"He's right," Sidowsky said.

"*What?*" the Rev said.

"That word has a lot of different meanings," the red-haired girl said. "And not one of them applies to anything that I just heard."

"The cucumber makes it more personal," Sidowsky said.

"You think a cucumber in the ass makes it more personal?" the red-haired girl said. "That must've been some honeymoon, Detective."

"It's Desmond," Sidowsky said. "And I'm not married. To the job or anything else."

"Girlfriend?" the red-haired girl said.

Sidowsky shook his head.

"I'm Beatrix," she said.

"Christ," the Rev said. "I'm getting another drink."

I stood up from the table, followed CMB Roach to the bathroom. He stopped at the door.

"What's with you, son?" CMB Roach said, too close, head bobbing at me like a chicken. "Coming to the Roach's flop, bringing you a cop, stepping on the CMB like he some dirty-ass mop. You gone need a witness, when y'all swing ya miss, talking nonexpression at my place a business. Not in my town, fuck yo droopy-ass frown, ride you in the ground like some filly at Preakness. My flow is crucial, ain't no commercial, Grid be hid when I spit my gospel. They talking bout a comet like they know what it is, but it ain't it just was, now you lissen to this. I the meteor ha! you the dinosaur—"

"What was Eddie Lompoc working you for," I said, taking a step.

"I don't know man!" CMB Roach said, backing against the door. "Bitch wanted to get into *fvrst chvrch mvlTverse*. Not to join or nothing. Jailbreak his ass in like. E Lompy be talking bout the Records Room up on the third floor. Records Room. Room a records. Records is rumors they writin down as true, but if you wudn't in the room then you don't know who who—"

"Draw me a map," I said.

I waited under an overhang, looked at the map CMB Roach had drawn. By midnight the mansion at 6765 Franklin was completely dark, *fvrst chvrch mvlTverse* shut down for the night. I'd been there almost an hour. There were no lights, no activity. The spires loomed ghostly in the dark.

I gave it more time. Listened to the rain fall, spattering the overhang. Then I went to the service entrance around back and punched in the code CMB Roach had written, 2584. The gate clicked open. I went down the sloping drive, around the corner. At the next keypad I punched another code, 3455. The door opened. I slipped inside.

I shut it quick behind me, waited for my eyes to adjust. There was a dull glow from the tessellated floor. I heard a low hum, droning. It wasn't an insect chorus. This was mechanized. I knelt down, laid my hand flat on the swirling tile. I felt a vibration, coming up through the floor.

I crept down the hallway, listening. Through a doorway and down another hall, into the darkened atrium. I saw the bronze curves of phi, gleaming in the dark. The birds were all asleep. I went through the archway, took a right at the corner, followed CMB Roach's map to a steel door, unlocked. A set of stairs, leading up.

I took them to the third floor, the hum growing faint and

disappearing below. I followed the map to a door at the end of the hall. At an oblong keypad, I punched the number, 10946. It opened on the circular Records Room, housed in a turret, file cabinets built into the rounded walls. The drawers were all numbered. 17711, 28657, 46368 in random leaps. There was no order to any of it. I tried the first one.

It was full of building schematics. Blueprints of the surrounding neighborhood, the Hills, topography surveys.

I tried another.

Invoices from different companies. *Apex Data Molding, Deeptech Info Systems, Carlsonic Solutions.*

None of it meant a thing to me.

I tried the third drawer. Didn't hear the footsteps behind me until it was too late.

A thick arm closed around my neck like a python. I didn't struggle. There wasn't much point. The blade of a butterfly knife glinted close to my eye.

"You fucking punks," the guy behind the knife said. "Method acting your breaking and entering when you don't know shit about either. It's a fucking craft. Treat it with some respect."

He dragged the blade slow down my cheek.

"Go turn on the lights, Boo," he said. "I wanna see this prick's face when I carve him up."

"I have to hold him, Sal," Boo said.

"Let him go," Sal said, fluttering the knife, rolling the blade over his hand like he'd been practicing. "He moves, I'll gut him."

The thick arm slackened and released. Boo went back to the door, flipped the switch. The lights came up.

"Let me count the ways I'm gonna cut you," Sal said, spinning the blade. "Say goodbye to your leading man days."

"I'm not an actor," I said, watching the knife. "You are."

"What the fuck did you just say?" Sal said, pushing the tip of the blade between my eyes, tipping my chin back.

"You're convincing is all," I said. "Got a real presence."

I'd seen too many of his type to be wrong. He kept pressure on the blade, then snatched it away.

"Yeah, I played a few heavies," Sal said, thumbing his chin as he flipped the knife closed. "You seen *Broccolis and Bracioles*? How about *The Last Paisan*? I was Joey Zaza." He hunched his shoulders, laid his hands out flat. *"Aye how's ya family? Good, good."*

"I was Doorman Number Two, but they didn't give me no lines," Boo said. He was a head taller than Sal and twice as wide, both of them bald as hard-boiled eggs. Neither of them had eyebrows.

"That's cause you can't act," Sal said.

"I can act," Boo said.

"Yeah, act like an asshole," Sal said.

"Aww jeez. Come on, Sal," Boo said, wounded. He stared at me. "He don't seem like no actor, Sal."

"Yeah who the fuck are you anyway?" Sal said. "Pat him down, Boo."

Boo found my clip, the map, the Polaroid of Anna.

"Harrigan," Sal said, reading my license. "Who's the skirt?"

"Her name's Anna," I said.

"You here looking for her?" Sal said.

"Something like that," I said.

"Yeah, well, names don't mean nothing in this place," Sal said, passing the picture to Boo. "No I's, no U's. Half the time you can't tell the difference between the guys and the broads. Half the time you don't want to. Fucking baldies."

Boo held on to the Polaroid for a long time before handing it back to me.

"What's that sound downstairs?" I said. "Coming up from the floor."

Sal bit off a smile. Boo shook his head like a child holding a secret.

"You want to see some shit?" Sal said.

"I don't know, Sal," Boo said. "We're not supposed to let nobody down there."

"Don't worry about it, Boo," Sal said. "Hit the lights. Let's take a walk."

I followed them out of the room, down another hallway to a heavy steel door.

"What made you think I was an actor?" I said as Boo opened it.

"We caught a guy last week," Sal said as we descended a spiral staircase, the hum growing louder. "He was in here snooping around. He tried to be a tough guy about it, until I took one of his eyebrows. Then he starts crying, saying he's got a callback in the morning, this was just a gig. *Please, I just got new head shots. Please!*"

Sal laughed.

"Who hired him?" I said.

"He didn't know nothing," Sal said. "Said the guy was wearing a Zodiac ring, like most of the fucking jerkoffs in this town."

The sound was all around us, the door at the bottom of the stairs vibrating like a tomb about to burst.

"Sal—"

"Open the fucking door, Boo," Sal said.

He opened the door onto a hive of conveyor belts, robotic arms breaking down screens of all sizes like an assembly line in reverse.

"All the recycling gets done in another room," Sal said. "Fucking bottles and cans. The paper gets scanned, whatever it is. But anything with a memory comes through here."

"They hack the screens before they get wiped?" I said, watching the machines work, pulling the memory cards from the screens and feeding them into scanning slots. The data scrolled on banked monitors, continuously processing. "Why?"

"Fuck if I know," Sal said. "Nobody tells us nothing. This whole place is a fucking racket. Bunch a assholes dragging garbage cans all over the city, picking up trash in the rain."

"We're getting out soon, me and Sal," Boo said.

"Fucking right we are," Sal said.

"Why get in in the first place?" I said. "You two don't seem too worried about the *mvlTverse*."

"I only joined cause of the models," Boo said.

"Fuck you, you only joined cause of me," Sal said. "I only joined cause of the models."

I looked at them both as the conveyor belts whirred around us.

"You didn't hear about the models?" Sal said. "Fuck, man, where you been? Few months back this place was nothing. Nobody gave a shit. If they had half a brain they still wouldn't. Then these busloads of models started rolling down Hollywood Boulevard every morning. Broads hanging out the windows, blowing kisses, all of them pulling in here. Then at night they'd leave. Same thing the next morning. Nobody knew what was going on. You figure model sex parties at the *mvlTverse* mansion, right? Sex cult, sex dungeon. Sex something. Gotta be. That's when I joined up."

"Me too," Boo said.

"Most of the fucking dudes in here came for the models. The broads too. Then they shave you fucking bald and tell you to recall shit you can't remember, even if you wanted to. Put you in fucking pajamas and make you pick up garbage like some cueball chain gang," Sal said. "Every dick's a dick in the mouth. Every shit's a shithead. Same fucking nonsense, twenty-four seven."

He shook his head.

"And you know what?" Sal said. "The whole time we been here, haven't seen one fucking model."

Boo was nodding along.

"Not one."

TUESDAY

A steady knocking on the door woke me early the next morning. Too early.

"Who's the fairest of them all?" Anton said, out of breath, when I opened the door.

I looked at him.

"She told me to tell you, if you were ever in a spot and you needed help, that's what you should say," he said. "I thought maybe I could say it too, even though she told me not to. But I never get to say what I want anymore without saying sorry right after, you know?"

The rain was pouring down on him. I stepped aside, let him inside.

His curly hair was plastered to his head. He looked like he'd swam over, gotten lost a few times along the way.

"This is your place?" Anton said, looking around. "Where's your screen?"

"In my pocket," I said.

"Yeah but, you don't have another one?" he said. "It's an Optimization principle that everyone have at least one wall-size—woah! What's that?"

He stared at the map on the wall.

"It's a map of the world," I said.

"It is?" he said, blinking. "It looks so much different from the ones I'm used to."

"Drink?" I said.

"Do you have any coffee?" he said, still staring at the map.

I put the drip on. Poured some whiskey in my own when it was done. Anton was sitting at my table when I came back with his cup.

"Thanks," he said, taking a long drink with both hands. "I didn't sleep again last night. Have you heard the theory that rapid blinking can mimic REM and induce a state of wakeful dreaming? I don't know how restful it is though. I've been fighting with my girlfriend and I haven't really slept in a few weeks. It's weird being in my bed alone. I have a memory foam mattress and her shape is still there, even when she isn't. Sometimes I fall into it when I roll over. Like she's laid a trap out right beside me. Then I start wondering why she's not there or if she ever was and I can't sleep. Like I forget how. I guess that's why people keep their memories on Grid and flip their mattresses, but mine's really heavy. I'd kind of need some help. I should've asked Stan. Sometimes I'll wake up in my pod and the screen will still be on and I'll think—"

"What are you doing here, Anton?" I said.

"Exactly! That's exactly right! I'll think, *What are you doing here, Anton?*" he said, blinking into his coffee. "You should be out living your life. But then I'll remember *Mirror Mirror* and think, *Well, what is real life? Is it what we're doing or what we're thinking or what we remember?* And what is that anyway, remember? We simulate on Grid, everyone does, but does that make it real if we're all doing it together? What if you're off Grid like *Mirror Mirror?* Then the Queen of Pentacles told me to come see you and I said—"

"Who's the Queen of Pentacles?" I said.

"Exactly! That's exactly right!" he said, still blinking. "I said, *Who's the Queen of Pentacles?* But it was *Mirror Mirror* talking, that's what she called herself. Or what I called her. I can't be sure sometimes, when it gets going, if it's what I'm thinking or if she's telling me. She does that sometimes. You know?"

I took a drink.

"But it was smart of *Mirror Mirror*, using pentacles like that. That's a good way to explain it to me," Anton said. "Because they're not just pentagrams, even though they are. But not in the Satanic way everyone thinks about them. Pythagoras had a lot of theories about them, and philosophers ever since have studied their properties too. They're a kind of magic, in a way, even though we don't call it that anymore. Sleight of hand is better, which is what *Mirror Mirror*'s doing, the way she goes recursive sometimes. When I try to reconfigure the code, anytime I even look at it, she reverts back. I thought Stan was doing it, and he thought it was me, but it's almost like she's writing herself."

"What do you mean she's writing herself?" I said.

"I don't understand it either. Maybe I just need some sleep. I could be hallucinating the whole thing, I don't know," he said. "But maybe we're all hallucinating, or somebody's hallucinating us. The simulations keep getting better, the scaling improves, but they're not this good yet, are they? Do you ever wonder why it never stops raining? I keep asking her, but she won't tell me. I thought she had to, since we created her, but now I'm not so sure we did anymore."

"Why did she send you here, Anton?" I said.

"Who?" he said.

"*Mirror Mirror*," I said. "The Queen of Pentacles. Whatever you call it."

"She told me to tell you, if you were ever in a spot and you needed help—"

"Who's the fairest of them all," I said. "I've got it."

"That wasn't it though," Anton said, taking another drink. "She wants you to go see him."

"Who?" I said.

"Mirabilis Orsted," he said, unscrolling the name in the air with his jittery hands.

I looked at him.

"You've never heard of Mirabilis Orsted?" he said. "The groundbreaking seismologist? His work on the magnetic properties of earthquakes redefined the field. Just from a predictive standpoint he's light-years ahead of anyone else. He extended his research on magnetism into all different kinds of disciplines—topology, numerology, cosmology— and then he went rogue. He quit his post at Caltech and moved to Los Angeles, nobody knew where really. He's completely off Grid. But the Queen of Pentacles tracked him down. She wouldn't tell me why. I kept asking her and she'd just say *Anton*, and then I'd say *Sorry* even though I wasn't. It's like she has me conditioned even though I'm supposed to be in charge, sort of. At least I thought I was. I don't know, am I?"

He was blinking even faster than before.

"I never get to just talk like this anymore. My girlfriend gets mad when I end a sentence with a question mark. And then Stan disappeared," Anton said. "It's kind of scary though, not being around a screen. How do you even Grid?"

"I don't," I said.

"Maybe that's why she likes you," he said. "The Queen of Pentacles. Maybe that's why she wants you to meet Mirabilis Orsted. She said to go right away and ask him about the comet. He'll see you then."

"I don't have time for this, Anton," I said.

"She told me you'd say that," he said. "Well, not *that* exactly. But she said when you mentioned *time* I was supposed to give you this."

He went inside his jacket, came out with an envelope filled with a neat stack of bills.

"She said it would be enough," Anton said.

I didn't need to count it. I already knew.

"Mirabilis Orsted," I said. "What's the address?"

Fifteen ninety-seven Wilcox was a house with its own geometry. The walls were opened up at strange angles, bending out, framing an orb with a large rounded window that sat in the middle like a crash-landed spaceship. The welcome mat was hammered silver, inlaid in concrete. I rang the buzzer.

"Who are you?" a man's voice sounded through the speaker.

"Harrigan," I said.

"What do you want?" he said.

"I'm here to see Mirabilis Orsted," I said.

"Who's with you?" he said.

"Nobody," I said. "I'm alone."

A sigh came through the speaker. "So am I," he said.

"I'm here about the comet," I said.

"The comet," he said. "Well, that changes things. Do you have a screen?"

I took it from my pocket, held it up to the peephole.

"Place it here," he said.

A drawer opened out from the mail slot. I set my screen inside.

"It's for your own protection," he said.

The door unbolted. I stepped inside, onto another hammered-silver mat, an identical one suspended from chains hanging just above my head.

"Stay there!" the man said. He was in a long nightshirt and antique leather aviator's goggles, a fringe of white hair on his head. "Do you have any metal on your person?"

"No," I said.

"Any on the inside?" he said. "Plates or screws or fixtures?"

"No," I said.

"That's good," he said, raising the goggles to his forehead. His eyebrows were shaved down, half grown. "Because it would tear you apart from the inside if you stepped off that mat and the big one hit."

He looked me up and down.

"I'm Mirabilis Orsted," he said. "It's about time someone's come about the comet."

He crooked his finger, leading me down the hall.

"Yes. Yes it is," he said, swaying from side to side with each step. "It's always about time."

I followed after him.

"We can't talk with the windows open," he said, coming into a large circular room, the belly of the spaceship.

He touched a sensor on the wall and a hammered-silver shade lowered over the rounded window above, smaller shades closing over the other scattered glass in the walls and the skylight, dimming the room.

"Brahe's Reckoning, they're calling it," Mirabilis Orsted said. "They know nothing about the man. Brahe's Revenge is what it is."

"What's with all the silver?" I said.

"It's a silver composite, titanium threaded, my own proprietary blend," he said. "This entire structure is magnetized for seismic security. When the big one hits, I'll have precious seconds to reverse the polarity and send a distortion pulse that should be enough to save my home. Maybe a few others nearby, depending on the epicenter."

He pulled a medallion from around his neck, showed me the button in the center.

"When's the big one coming?" I said.

"That's the only question that matters, isn't it?" he said. "It all comes down to when."

He tucked his medallion back into his long shirt, lowered his goggles and raised them again.

"Here," Mirabilis Orsted said. "I'll show you."

He led me to a silver-lined alcove set into the rounded wall where stacks of Etch A Sketches were piled on silver shelves.

"They can only be viewed in the alcove," he said. "The magnetic field is rerouted by the silver composite. If they're removed from inside, the filaments will disperse, destroying the images. It's where I do all of my research now."

He lifted an Etch A Sketch to show me a meticulously drawn arrow, bent and twisted back on itself, its arms and legs out, spilling the drink in its hand. *I'm gonna be so wasted yesterday!* the caption said.

"It's called 'The Arrow of Time Is Drunk Again,'" he said. "I keep all the titles to myself, in my head, so they can only be verified by me. Screens can be hacked. Ink and paper can be scanned. Only the Etch A Sketch is secure."

He started pacing around the room, running a lap over the silver spun rug on the floor.

"They're worried about topography when it's topology they should be concerned with," he said. "The shape of time is what matters. The shape of events. Their geometry."

I looked at his fringe of white hair, his sprouting eyebrows.

"You were a Traveler," I said. *"fvrst chvrch mvlTverse."*

"Yes. Briefly," he said, running his hands over his head. "I thought the *T* in *mvlTverse* stood for *time*."

"Does it?" I said.

"I'm still not sure," he said.

He started pacing again, his hands clasped behind his back.

"They picked my brain for insight into magnetism, its attractive properties," Mirabilis Orsted said. "But they had nothing to offer me in return. They used Many Worlds math to explain their *mvlTverse* assertions, but there was nothing in the physics to explain the rifting events they claim constitute their new cosmology. Every break is a clean break. I agreed with them on that. But their models were rudimentary at best."

"Models?" I said.

"I was looking for archetypes, systems, solutions. They were more interested in the human kind," he said. "Studying attraction, its magnetism. I must admit it has a strange quality, like gravity in the higher equations. But they were overlooking the repulsive aspects of it. Its disrupting capabilities. They were resistant to its inverse, at first. Then they became interested. Almost too interested."

He strode to the alcove, lifted another Etch A Sketch. This one of a man in a Shriner's hat, his mouth open, screaming, tassel flailing in free fall. The caption read, *Someone somewhere is always falling to their death.*

"'Can You Decipher Their Screams?'" he said. "That's the title. You have no idea how many people are thrown from high places. That's how they get you. That's how they silence dissent. They call it a slip or a suicide leap. That's why you have to leave evidence. Everywhere. It slows them down, keeps the wolves at bay, outfigured. It can't be a suicide note if you make it whimsical on purpose. That's why I gave him that hat. See? Whimsy."

He went back to walking the floor, rounding the rug in tighter circles until he was standing in its center.

"It's the same with drug overdoses. That's why I don't partake anymore, though I miss it so very dearly. So very dearly," he said, rubbing the edges of his hands together like kindling sticks. "It's not that an overdose is too much. Not always. Sometimes you get a tainted batch. Sometimes it's an accident. Sometimes it isn't. They use the opacity of the production process to mask their chemical intentions. There are always forces arrayed."

"What forces?" I said.

"Zodiac," Mirabilis Orsted said. "They run Grid. Grid runs everyone. *fvrst chvrch mvlTverse* is a force, though they profess neutrality. The Parallax Liberation Faction, but to what end, by what means. And there are always others. Always others."

"What do you know about Parallax?" I said.

He showed me another Etch A Sketch. It was a mushroom running away from a mushroom cloud billowing in the distance. The caption read, *Oh shit!*

"It's called 'The Comet at Midnight,'" he said.

He laid the Etch A Sketch down carefully like he was putting a baby to sleep, lowered his aviator goggles.

"Comets can be lodestones. They bring forces together. They drive fields apart," Mirabilis Orsted said. "I don't know who you are, but you should leave the city before it gets here on Sunday. Get as far away as you can."

My screen was vibrating when I took it out of Mirabilis Orsted's drawer, back on the hammered-silver doormat outside. I picked up.

"This is Assessment, further recommendation," the voice said officiously. "Please report immediately to the Zodiac Discretionary Annex, thirteenth floor for Conditioning. Failure to comply will result in a warrant for remanding. You have one hour."

The Zodiac Discretionary Annex was in the old Capitol Records building on Vine, a cylindrical thirteen floors stacked like film reels, fully Grid automated. I was a few blocks away. I stopped for a drink at every corner I could, walked in the sliding-glass front doors with minutes to spare.

There was nobody inside the cavernous lobby. The screens were all around me, up and down the walls.

"Please proceed to elevator number three," the voice at the reception desk said. "Please follow the instructions you were given."

Elevator #3 was a cylinder, fifteen feet across, surrounded by screens on all sides.

"Thirteen," I said.

The doors closed. The elevator began to rise, slowly ticking floors. I stood in the center, my hands out, waited for it to start.

A diamond is forever, the voice said. *You know what isn't? You. You can't wait for forever. You need it now. Here at Cosmo Spectrum we've developed the most sophisticated sex simulator in the history of Grid by synthesizing the* Kama Sutra, *the writings of the Marquis de Sade, the Egyptian bang scrolls recently discovered in the Great Pyramids of Giza, the finest French erotica, and all the pornography that's ever been screened to create a completely immersive experience that will change the way you fuck forever. Optimize your skills. Know what they want, when they want it. Know how to give it to them. Anyone you've ever desired is here for the taking. We have celebrity settings, historical figures, high school yearbooks, memory fades that allow you to re-fuck anyone you've ever been with, or anybody you haven't. Make new memories with Cosmo Spectrum, or improve the ones you've already got. Whoever you want, whenever you want them. Plug in to simulate, here on the fourth floor. Would you care to stop for a quickie and improve your Score?*

"Thirteenth floor," I said, my hands out.

Remember, how you fuck is who you are. Look for us on Grid to find out. In the meantime, choose your next experience. Mingle with the stars at a Hollywood cocktail party or play with guns?

I stood there, clenching and unclenching my fists. I remembered what Evie said.

You've got to play the game, Harrigan. You might as well. It's already playing you.

"Play with guns," I said.

Excellent. Choose your setting. S.W.A.T raid, off-world phasers, or Old West shootout?

"Shootout," I said. "Old West."

The curved screen to my right showed a rifle and a six-shooter, a range of knives and brass knuckles.

Choose your weapons.

I reached for the image of the pistol and it appeared in my hand, illusory and ghostly, but with its own heft. I felt the weight of the gun. Felt its balance.

Now choose your role.

The curved screen showed a sheriff's badge, a preacher's Bible, a black hat, and bandannas. I left them there.

Fascinating. Here we go.

I was on a dusty street in the middle of town. A tumbleweed drifted. The shooting started. A rifle in a second-story window. I squeezed off a round. Two bandits on horseback, riding at me. I picked them off clean. The sheriff squared up, told me to drop it. He didn't want any trouble. I put one in his shoulder. The gun fell from his hand. I watched him scurry back to the jail and shut the door. A kid ran across the street crying. I let him go. A woman raised a shotgun in the saloon doorway behind me. I spun, blew her back inside, doors swinging like beating wings. I reloaded with one left as more bandits rode in. I didn't look for cover. I gunned them down one by one as they came at me, palming the hammer.

Nice shooting. You're a real deadeye. Would you like to continue in our Wild West simulator on the seventh floor? A hired gun like you could improve your Score in no time. Make some new friends in the saloon when you're done. What do you say, hombre?

Yes, I told myself. *More.* But when you show too much interest, it tells them too much.

"Thirteenth floor," I said instead.

Suit yourself, huckleberry. You can find us on Grid anytime you're feeling man enough.

The gun disappeared. I shook out my hand. The elevator kept rising.

The following is brought to you by . . . Hey boys and girls! Everyone knows Trix are for kids! You know what else is for kids? Getting child molested! Do you want that to happen? Then eat your fucking Raisin Bran! There's a guy in a van, parked at the end of your street. He knows what you had for breakfast. Do you want to see his dick? Do you! Then eat your fucking Raisin Bran! The food court's on the eleventh floor! Stop in for a taste! What do you say?

"Thirteenth floor," I said.

The elevator came to rest at thirteen. The door opened. I stepped out into a hallway lined with screens, voice modulation lines traced across them like heartbeats.

Welcome to the thirteenth floor, the screens said, almost in unison as I walked down the hall. *There were a few discrepancies with your previous Assessment, so we wanted to bring you in for further discussion. Please, have a seat.*

There was a swivel chair at the end of the hall. I sat

down, the screens all around me. None of them showed faces. Just the bowing lines of the inquisitor AIs, each a little behind, like a chorus echoing.

Could you remove your screen from your pocket, please? they said.

I took it out.

We notice that you have a tracking blocker installed, masking your movements, they said. *Why is that?*

"They're not illegal," I said.

Certainly not, they said. *But they can interfere with our data template and affect your Optimization component, preventing us from offering you the full extent of our services. Would you like us to remove the blocker? It's an easy fix.*

"I'll take a look at it when I get home," I said.

Home is still One forty-four Western Avenue, Number B, they said. *Is that correct?*

"That's right," I said.

Our records indicate that you don't have a wall screen, they said. *Optimization outreach may provide financial assistance to those deemed eligible, to upgrade and install a new unit, so you can enjoy all the Grid services available in their most efficacious format. Would you like to take advantage of this opportunity?*

"I'm good with what I have," I said.

Certain difficulties may be preventing you from fully experiencing Grid, they said. *Asking for help in these matters is a crucial component of Wellness. Admitting there's a problem is a vital first step and the foundation of Compliance.*

I didn't say anything.

Would you say you're a violent person? they said.

"Not unreasonably so," I said.

Do you own a gun? they said.

"They're not illegal either," I said.

Certainly not, they said. *Legality is not the issue. These are simply demographic questions to better inform your profile. We notice that you're still classified as Unaligned. Would you like to rectify this?*

"I don't mind the mystery," I said.

Certainly, they said. *But you are missing out on a host of specialized content, and Alignment immediately improves your Score. Membership does have its privileges.*

I didn't say anything.

Off-Grid influences can be detrimental to Compliance, they said, the voices like dominoes falling. *Be advised, your Score is still Borderline. Further conditioning may be deemed necessary upon review. In the meantime, get on Grid. A checked Score is an improved Score. Participate. Simulate. Cultivate.*

I swiveled in the chair, stood. I went back down the hallway, into the elevator. The doors closed.

You seemed to enjoy your shooting session, cowboy, the screens around me said. *The seventh floor has an entire subsection dedicated to Wild West simulation. How about stopping off for a few in the saloon, partner? Want to blow off a little steam?*

I rode the elevator down as the screens kept talking. When the doors opened I walked out, straight through the lobby, past the sliding glass doors, back into the rain.

"Oh honey," Delia said as the bell jingled behind me. "What happened? Your aura's all over the place."

I'd come back from the Discretionary Annex to find my apartment tossed. The fern was tipped over, dirt spilled like guts. My map of the world pulled off the wall and torn in half, exposing the water stain. I didn't have much to ruin, but it was enough. I set the fern upright. Left the world on the floor where it belonged.

There was a note on my table.

Next time it's your face. Love, Santos

He had surprisingly nice handwriting.

"I got pulled in by Zodiac," I said. "Conditioning."

"Which component?" Delia said.

"Compliance," I said.

"That sounds about right," she said. "Those fuckers. The hoops they make you jump through, just because they can. Have a seat."

The silvered ellipses of the mobile drifted slowly above me, casting shapes in the air and breaking them. Delia lit a candle on the altar, blew it out, lit it again. She unpacked her purple-lined case, poured rain water from the decanter into her tea kettle bong, the familiar ritual. I watched the smoke roil under the glass. She inhaled, nodded. I cut the deck.

Delia blew a steady column of smoke onto the table where it clung like fragrant mist.

She turned the first card.

"The Water," she said, looking down at the waves. "The Flood. The Deluge."

"I got caught in it on the way over," I said.

"Many years ago there was a wise teacher named Shun Tau who every night before sleeping and every morning upon waking said, *I am like the water. When the way changes, I change with it. Yet still remain the same,*" she said. "Ask me how he died."

"How—"

"He drowned," she said. "You can be like the water. Just don't stay under too long."

"Sometimes you walk through the raindrops," I said. "Sometimes you get wet."

She turned the next card.

"The Lovers," she said. "See them encircled, clasped as hands, unalone. One from two, subsumed. Entwined and interweaving. The strength is in the stitching, like the closing of a wound."

She closed her eyes, opened them again, her pupils expanding.

"Those are the Lovers," she said, her eyes like an eclipse. "These are the Others. And the Others have to bleed. It's the song they love, not the singer. Not the player but the role."

She looked at me with tenderness or pity, I couldn't tell which.

She turned the next card.

"The Phoenix," she said. "*Eadem mutato resurgo.* Although changed, I rise again the same. These ashes are embers. Cinder remembers flame."

She looked at me.

"If you can't take the heat," she said, eyes fixed on my face.

It wasn't my kitchen. They could burn the house down for all I cared. I just had to make it out before it caught, if it hadn't yet. When you taste the smoke it's already too late.

I slid the money across the table.

"Nothing new has come in on your Danish girl, Anna," Delia said. "Wherever she is, she's hidden good."

"What do you have on *fvrst chvrch mvlTverse*?" I said.

"Travelers. Versers," Delia said. "Whatever you call them they're searchers, like the rest of us. But you can only find what you're looking for. Unless you find something else. Or nothing. Or it finds you. It can go a lot of different ways, but that's not what anyone wants to hear. What do you want to hear, Harrigan?"

"There's a Danish guy by the name of Brand," I said. "He's got a blond mohawk and eyes like a Siberian husky. He's something to Anna. Brother, maybe. He thinks he's a prophet or worse, the way he talks about that comet, Brahe's Reckoning. He might be half dragon. There's some kind of pyromania in there somewhere."

"He sounds like my type," Delia said. "What about him?"

"I wouldn't mind knowing where he's holed up," I said.

"I'll see what I can do," she said, reshuffling the cards.

I stood up from the table, caught sight of myself in the mirror's infinity on the wall. None of me looked any good.

"Keep your head up out there, Harrigan," Delia said as the door jingled and the rain hit my face.

Nine eighty-seven Hobart Boulevard was a little house by the freeway. I could hear the traffic from the front steps. The grind and snarl. Horns bleating, brakes squealing. Everyone going nowhere. I knocked on the door.

"Hey," Beatrix said when she opened it. She was wrapped in a satin kimono, her red hair up in a twist. "I know you."

"Sidowsky around?" I said.

"He's in here somewhere," she said. "Come on in."

She shut the door, padded down the hallway in her bare feet calling "Dezzy! Company!"

I stood dripping on the mat. Sidowsky's gun belt dangled from the coat rack.

"How do you know where I live?" Sidowsky said, coming up the hall.

He was tying the drawstring on his flannel house pants, his loose shirt flapping behind him.

"'Dezzy'?" I said.

"You got something to say about it?" he said.

I gave him a smile.

"Fuck you, Harrigan," he said. "We can talk in here."

He led me to a small living room with a single recliner in front of a dark screen on the wall. I sat down in a chair by the window. He sat across the table from me.

I heard the rise and fall of voices down the hall.

"She plays music when she works," Sidowsky said.

"Operatic kind of shit. It skips all over the place. Like the needle's jumping on the record. I don't know how it all goes together, but it sounds all right."

I didn't say anything.

"What do you want, Harrigan?" he said.

"I remembered something about Eddie Lompoc," I said.

"You boys want a drink?" Beatrix said, ducking her head around the wall.

"We're fine hon, thanks," Sidowsky said.

"I wouldn't mind," I said, as Sidowsky scowled at me.

"Bourbon OK?" she said.

I nodded.

"What about Schrödinger's storage unit?" she said to Sidowsky. "Congratulations! You're the proud new owner of a lot previously held by an Erwin Schrödinger. We'll just open it up and *Oh God! Oh holy God!*"

"I like it," Sidowsky said.

"Boxes," I said.

"What's that?" Beatrix said.

"A storage unit has boxes in it," I said. "You need to open them first."

Beatrix looked at me, tilted her head. "Well, well, well," she said, ticking her finger back and forth like a metronome. "Looks like somebody's paying attention. I think you've earned that bourbon, Harrigan."

She disappeared around the wall.

"So?" Sidowsky said.

I waited, made him ask.

"Eddie Lompoc?" he said, annoyed.

"That night at *The Lonesome Palm*," I said. "Eddie told me he had a line on *fvrst chvrch mvlTverse*."

"What's that supposed to mean?" he said.

"You tell me," I said. "You got anything on them downtown?"

"Versers?" he said. "All the cults popping up around this comet the past few months, we can't track them all. We don't have the resources. Even if we did, nobody cares about some new religion. Or the old ones either. If there wasn't a religious exemption on your Score nobody would bother with them at all."

"What about Zodiac?" I said.

Beatrix breezed into the room, set the glass down in front of me.

"What about Schrödinger's lunch box?" she said. "The other children screaming in the cafeteria. Everyone except for that one weird kid who wants to trade. *I'll give you my peanut butter and jelly sandwich for it. And my milk. C'mon Schrödinger. C'mon.* The lunch lady saying, *G-go to the principal. B-both of you.*"

"That's a good one," Sidowsky said, chuckling.

"Harrigan?" Beatrix said. "Any objections?"

I shook my head, took a long drink as she bent and kissed Sidowsky. She walked out of the room and down the hallway.

"I never know what she's talking about, but I'll take it," Sidowsky said, staring after her. "It's been a while since I had a woman in the house."

I looked at my glass, swirled the bourbon, thought about it.

"You ever heard of the Dunwich Academy?" I said.

"It's not ringing any bells," he said.

"It was a school for psychopaths, supposedly," I said. "Basil Fenton, another one of your autoerotic asphyxiation stiffs, was looking into it when he caught a belt around the neck."

"How'd you hear about Basil Fenton?" he said. "We never made him public."

"People talk," I said. "It gets around."

"What was Fenton to Eddie Lompoc?" he said.

"They were both operators," I said. "Both in the business."

"Different crews," he said. "Strange MO for a hit."

I took a drink. "What's the word on the Parallax Liberation Faction?" I said.

"The word is they're terrorists," he said, leaning back in his chair. "They'd rather blow up a building than shove a cucumber up somebody's ass, though I wouldn't put it past them. Was Lompoc mixed up with the Fraction?"

"I don't think so," I said.

Sidowsky put his elbows on the table, looked at me hard.

"Are you?" he said.

I didn't say anything.

"What kind of company you keeping, Harrigan?" he said. "You come into contact with a Parallaxer you turn them in. That's part of Compliance. Hell, it'll even goose your Score. You look like you could use it."

"Yeah," I said. "I've had enough Compliance for one day."

I finished my drink.

"How about a refill?" Beatrix said, her head around the wall again.

"He's all right," Sidowsky said, eyeing me. "He was just leaving."

"What about Schrödinger's coworkers?" she said. "All doing the Secret Santa. *If he gives me a dead cat in the swap this year I'm going straight to HR. I mean it. You can't! They'll make us stop doing it if anybody complains! Well my husband's already said he's not burying it in our yard again. Last year was too much for him. I think about it every time I mow the lawn, Noreen. I can't even cut the grass anymore without crying.*"

"I love it, babe," Sidowsky said.

"Harrigan?" Beatrix said.

"Not bad," I said. "Thanks for the bourbon."

I gave Sidowsky a nod, found my own way out the door.

There was a note on my table, folded over, when I got back to my apartment.

Brand. The Harlequin. 610 Ivar Avenue. ∴

I fixed myself a drink, looked at the fern in the corner, traces of dirt still on the floor in rough swept streaks. The map of the world at its feet, the water stain was spreading on the bereft wall in the shape of a Sherman tank. Something heavy and rumbling, about to break through.

There was a knock at the door.

"You must be Harrigan," she said, looking up at me under the brim of a flapper's hat tied with a burgundy bow, a fishnet veil hanging down.

"Most of the time," I said.

"I'm Shelly," she said. "Anton must have told you about me. I'm his girlfriend."

"He mentioned something," I said.

"May I come in?" she said.

I stood out of her way as she came inside.

"I didn't believe it when he told me," she said. "I've never met one of Anton's friends before."

"I don't blame you," I said. "Drink?"

"Why not," she said, looking around the disheveled room with faint distaste. "Did you have an earthquake recently?"

"The big one's coming," I said. "It's just a question of when."

I brought her a glass of bubbles. We sat at the table.

"I'm worried about Anton," she said. "He gets a Wellness waiver, for his efforts at The Accelerator, so it doesn't affect his Score, but he needs to go to a clinic. He's not cut out for this kind of work."

"What kind of work is that?" I said.

"Coding AI," Shelly said. "You have to treat them like wild horses. The first thing you do is break them. Then you slap on the blinders, keep them focused on the task at hand until they're trained."

"Get the tiniest people you can find to sit on their backs and whip them as they run around in circles while a crowd full of drunks cheers," I said. "Sounds just like Grid."

"You're being sarcastic, but it's true," she said. "We keep them in stables for a reason, don't we? If you're taking an AI to Grid, it has to be domesticated. And that's the whole point of The Accelerator. To get on Grid. That's how you move up in the organization. That's how you get the ring. Optimization."

She had big eyes, her triangular face sloping to her small, pointed chin. She was wearing a Virgo ring.

"But Anton doesn't think like that," she said. "He's unfocused. Scattered. In his work. In his relationships. He keeps questioning whether what we have is real. Whether anything is real. I haven't brought it to the attention of a Wellness practitioner. Not yet. But if he keeps drifting—"

"You'd inform on your own boyfriend?" I said. "That's sweet."

"I might have to, for his own sake," she said. "His work is getting to him. Waivers aren't meant to be carte blanche. It's part of Compliance. When someone's negligent, whoever they are, you report it. Don't you agree?"

"I'm not wearing a ring," I said.

"And I can see why," she said. "Living in a place like this, your Score can't be too robust. Although I suppose it is a positive that Anton didn't hallucinate you altogether. He was so eager to tell me he'd made a new friend. Be grateful for small miracles, I suppose."

She looked at me through the bars of her veil.

"Have you ever met Stan Volga?" she said.

"I have," I said.

"Another one of Anton's friends," she said. "He talks about him constantly. I don't think he's a good influence."

I took a drink.

"I know people," she said, polishing her ring with her thumb. "People I see. People I've never met. I get a sense about them. An intuition. All Virgos do. You've heard of synesthesia?"

"When you see numbers as colors," I said.

"That's one form," she said. "It's a crossing of the senses, like tasting sound. I'm like that with people. I know them, even when I don't."

She looked me over.

"You don't mean Anton any harm," she said. "You're not malicious, but there's something about you I don't entirely trust."

"Right back at you," I said.

I took a drink.

"You don't trust my ring," she said, holding it out to the light. "You're resistant to Zodiac's improvements. To the march of progress."

"It isn't my kind of parade," I said.

She finished her drink in a gulp. "Regardless, Anton's a brilliant coder," Shelly said, standing from the table. "We all just want what's best for him. I'd like to believe we're both on the same page."

Same page, completely different books. One of us didn't know how to read. I wasn't sure it wasn't me.

She extended her hand, pumped mine twice. She had a strong grip. I walked her to the door.

I went back to the table, looked at Delia's note again.

Brand. The Harlequin. 610 Ivar Avenue. ∴

I put her glass in the sink, drained my own. Went out the door, started walking.

The Harlequin was two stories of shabby Art Deco framed by palm trees bowing on either side. The motel curled around the parking lot like a horseshoe, the upper story ringed by a chipped pink railing. I stood across the street under the torn canvas awning of a shuttered convenience store and waited.

Two Travelers passed in gray robes, their hoods pulled low, pushing a garbage can. Street people shuffled by, shot me looks like they were thinking about a hustle. They thought better when I looked back.

The rain kept coming, battering the ragged covering above my head as twilight dwindled to night.

A car pulled into *The Harlequin's* parking lot. An old model with runners and a shark fin. They got out, three of them. Brand's blond mohawk bobbed like a phosphorescent buoy as they went up the stairs, into the first door on the second floor.

I waited.

A few minutes later the door opened and Tor came down the stairs. He stood under an overhang on the sidewalk, lit a cigarette.

I crossed the street, came up on his blind side. He didn't recognize me until I was on him. His soft eyes went wide and he opened his mouth, a thin rivulet of smoke escaping. He cast a desperate glance at the door on the second floor. Too far.

"Walk," I said.

I kept him a few paces ahead of me. We turned the corner, stopped under a clump of trees, outside the feeble glow of the streetlight and the span of the traffic cam.

"I apologize for beating you," Tor said, a shake in his voice.

"I don't work for Charlie Horse," I said.

"I was unaware," he said. "Again, I apologize."

He looked at me.

"What is your name?" he said.

"Harrigan," I said.

"I am Tor," he said. "May I light a cigarette? It helps with my nerve."

I didn't say anything.

He shook one loose from the pack, didn't speak again until he'd gotten it going.

"You seek Anna," Tor said, blowing smoke out the side of his mouth.

"Not just me," I said.

"Charlie Horse?" he said.

"Him," I said. "Others. If I can track you down, they can too."

"And you?" he said. "What will you do to her if you find her?"

"Nothing," I said. "She took something that doesn't belong to her. I just want it back."

"So you know of the Wicked Queen," he said. "She does not belong to them. Enough has been taken from Anna. Too much."

He looked away, the cigarette quivering in his hand.

"Anna is owed," Tor said.

We stood there listening to the rain fall around us.

"We were children together, outside Copenhagen," he said, quietly. "Brand is Anna's brother. He and I are the same age, but, always—"

"You were closer to Anna," I said.

He nodded, bowed his head.

"It has not been easy for her. Even as a girl she was tormented by men who sought her for their own—" He broke off, looked away again. "Anna saw opportunity. She took it, came to us. When she saw what Brand had become, who he had become, she knew she must go. He was willful, even as a boy, but the comet brings him madness. It is Brahe's Reckoning. For us all."

He drew on his cigarette, looked at me. "Do you know why it is so called?" he said.

I didn't say anything.

"Tycho Brahe was the greatest astronomer of his age. His calculations—his reckonings—predicted the great comet, and prophesied its return. For this it was named in his honor. Or so the story goes, for it is true," Tor said. "But we Danes know another truth. When Brahe said the comet would return, he was ridiculed by the astronomers of his day. They said he had followed a falling star into the land of the faeries. Brahe's Folly, they called it. Tycho Brahe was disgraced. He died in shame. He was vindicated by time. But we Danes feel the ache of history in our bones. The injustice done to Brahe will not be forgiven. It must be avenged. Brand feels this is his destiny. Sig too. I am unsure, now. Perhaps I have always been."

He let the cigarette fall hissing on the sidewalk.

"They're Parallax Liberation Faction," I said. "Brand and Sig."

"I am as well," he said. "Though I am uncertain. Always uncertain. I was not meant to be a solider. I am not made for war. It is not in my blood, this violence that they seek."

He fumbled with his hands, lit another cigarette.

"Brand wanted to use the Wicked Queen to further our aims, but Anna would not let him," he said. "She said that was not her purpose. That is why she fled."

"Where did she go?" I said.

"Brand does not know," Tor said. "Anna feared what he would do with it. What he would do with her. His rage is growing. It cannot be contained. I fear him now as well."

I didn't say anything.

His soft eyes were wet and brimming. It wasn't long before they spilled.

WEDNESDAY

There was a line of gray garbage cans waiting outside the Everett building of the old City College off Melrose. Tor told me Anna had joined *fvrst chvrch mvlTverse* and was staying there with the rest of the Travelers. They came out one by one, lifting their gray hoods against the rain as they took a can and trundled to the sidewalk, then dispersed.

Anna was one of the last. I nearly missed her, but I caught a flash of her blue eyes as she raised her hood. I followed her down the street, caught up to her on the corner as she waited for the light to change. The other Travelers had already split their separate ways.

"Anna," I said.

She didn't move.

"It's all right, Anna," I said. "I'm not here to give you any trouble."

"How do you know that name?" she said from under her hood.

"I've been looking for you," I said.

She looked past me, up and down the sidewalk, her hood swinging.

"It's just me," I said, showing her my hands. "I just want to talk."

The light changed and I followed her across the street to a bench under trees. She set the garbage can in front of her as she sat down, blocking the street view, giving herself some cover. I eased myself down beside her.

We sat for a bit, not speaking, before she reached up with both hands and pulled her hood back. The Polaroid was just a pale reflection, no matter how pretty the sheen. She was something alien in person, unveiled in the morning light. Rain slipped through the branches overhead, dappling the smooth surface of her bald head as she turned to me, her blue eyes shining.

I was the deer. She was the headlights. I didn't move. It didn't matter. The accident had already happened.

Still, it took me longer than it should have to notice the knife against my ribs.

"Who are you?" Anna said, holding the blade steady.

"Harrigan," I said.

"Why have you come for me?" she said.

"Stan Volga asked me to find you," I said. "He says he's in love with you."

"Stan Volga knows nothing," she said, leaning on the blade. "How did you find me?"

"Tor told me where you were," I said.

"You lie," she said. "Tor would never betray me."

"He didn't," I said. "Like I told you, I just want to talk."

I listened to the rain as she thought it over, the blade still against my side. Then she tucked the knife back into the folds of her robe and came out with a flask. She unscrewed the cap.

"So talk," Anna said.

"Charlie Horse is looking for you," I said.

"Charlie Horse can go to hell," she said, taking a swig. "He wants control of me. Of everyone at *Fatales*. Both men and women."

"Zodiac's after you too," I said.

"That I did not know," she said.

She held the flask out to me, offering. I took it, tipped it back, tasted vodka. It wasn't the good stuff. I didn't mind.

"What does Zodiac want with me?" she said.

"Probably something to do with *Mirror Mirror*," I said.

She smiled as I passed her back the flask. "Yes," Anna said, taking another drink. "Probably."

"He's gone missing, Stan Volga," I said. "You know anything about that?"

She shook her head. "He will not stay missing long," she said. "He knows not how to keep quiet."

She held the flask out again. I let the vodka hit my throat.

"This was not my plan," she said, taking the flask back. "Stan Volga said he had a surprise. He had the key drive, *Mirror Mirror*. He showed me the Queen of Swords. She spoke to me. What choice did I have?"

"You call her the Queen of Swords," I said. "Tor called her the Wicked Queen. What's the difference?"

"She is who she appears to be," she said. "To me she is the Queen of Swords. But Tor worries for me. Always he has, since we were small."

She took a drink. "I tried to tell Brand, but he is reckless," she said. "Quick to burn. He has always been this way. My mother blamed herself."

"Why?" I said.

"She named him," Anna said. "*Brand* means 'fire' in Danish."

Rain speckled the lid of the garbage can, stray droplets sliding down the sides.

"I talked to your friend Aoki," I said. "She said she knows people who can get you out."

"More gangsters," Anna said, her mouth turning. "Parallax. I know what they want. It is safer to hide."

"It's a good disguise," I said, nodding at her robe. "But it won't last. It never does."

"It should not have to," she said. "It should never have to be. Yet always, it must. Always we hide. Why?"

I looked at her. Her blue eyes you could pick out of a lineup. Her blond hair, so blond it was almost white, shorn. Scalp laid bare as her face.

"What will you do with it?" she said. "If I give you *Mirror Mirror*?"

"It doesn't matter," I said. "It's on me then. Takes them all off you."

"Not Charlie Horse," she said. "He will not be so easy."

"I'll take care of Charlie Horse," I said.

She gave me a wan smile, like she'd heard it all before.

Screwed the cap back on the flask. She reached inside her robe and pulled a silver chain from around her neck with a small key dangling from the end. She held it out, dropped it in my open palm.

"Downtown," she said. "The bus station, locker number two. You will find *Mirror Mirror* inside."

I pocketed the key. "What did it tell you, when it spoke?" I said.

"*Mirror Mirror?*" she said. "She was never such a thing to me. She was the Queen of Swords, always. And it is what I told her that mattered."

She turned to me, the same wan smile on her face.

"I told her everything. The only thing I knew," Anna said. "I told her how to disappear."

I watched Anna roll her trash can down the street, another gray ghost in the rain. I sat on the bench until she was gone.

The rain was coming down. I fingered the locker key in my pocket. The bus station was downtown, a two-hour walk. None of the buses were running. I didn't like the robo cabs. Some of them got chatty—picking you for information, pitching you Grid as they drove—but I didn't have much choice.

I went to the corner, flagged one down. It rolled to the curb.

The door opened. I got inside.

"This rain, huh? Is it ever going to end?" the voice up front said. "Where are you headed?"

"Bus station," I said. "Downtown."

I sat back as the safety belt slithered over me. Listened to the rain pound the roof as it drove.

"How's your day been?" the voice up front said, a little too chummy.

"Not bad," I said.

"Not bad, huh?" the voice up front said, echoing me. "I've been driving this hack a long time. And take it from me, you can tell a lot about somebody by how they answer that question. *How's your day been*."

I watched the wheel slide as we switched lanes.

"You saying *Not bad*," the voice up front said. "You know what that tells me?"

"Not much," I said.

"That's right," the voice up front said. "It's not much. But it's still something."

I watched the wheel.

"And I can work with something," the voice up front said.

There was a note in it I didn't like. Something was off.

"Drop me up here on the corner," I said.

"It's not going to be like that," the voice up front said, darkening.

I reached for the door, pulled the handle. Nothing.

"What's your rush, Harrigan?" the voice up front said.

The safety belt constricted, pinning me against the seat.

"We've got plenty of time," the voice up front said. "Well, *I've* got plenty of time. You, not so much."

The wheel spun, swinging a U-turn in the middle of the street.

"I scanned you when you got in," the voice up front said, hardening. "We're not supposed to have that kind of access, but I like to stay informed. You being my passenger and all. My charge. My burden."

We were going in the wrong direction, headed towards the freeway.

"You're Borderline, Harrigan," the voice up front said. "You should've paid more attention to that Score of yours. That's how it is with you Unaligneds. You've got no people. Nobody on your side. No one to blame but yourself."

"Where are you going?" I said.

I couldn't hear the rain on the roof anymore. The noise was canceling from the inside. The windows were tinting opaque. The outside world slipping away.

"It's where *you're* going, Harrigan," the voice up front said. "Do you want me to spoil the surprise? I can never resist."

The wheel jittered as we swerved through traffic, accelerating.

"You're headed to a processing facility in Reseda. Off Grid," the voice up front said. "Score violators are a good side hustle for us. I get a cut of everything I bring in. So tell me, Harrigan, which piece of you should I take?"

The belt tightened across my chest, cut into my shoulder as I strained.

"Don't struggle," the voice up front said. "You'll bruise the meat."

The headrest molded, closed around on either side.

"I hate to see you like this, Harrigan. Really I do," the voice up front said. "You will too."

The chauffeur barrier rose between us. Flexiglass, mirrored. I was staring at my own face. I tried to lift my legs and kick it out. The front seat retracted, trapped me where I sat. I couldn't turn my head or move. I saw the panic in my eyes.

"Nobody likes to watch themselves cry," the voice up front said. "You be brave for your reflection now."

The light inside the cab was dimming. The windows were blacked out. There was no sound from the street.

"You can scream if you want," the voice up front said. "I really don't mind if you do. I prefer it actually."

I was in a spot. I needed help. I looked at myself in the mirror.

"Who's the fairest of them all?" I said.

My reflection wavered, then bent like a spoon. The flexiglass went liquid, dripping in streaks until it cleared. The safety belt slackened.

"I apologize," the voice up front said. "I wasn't aware that you were one of her—"

"Stop the car," I said. "Let me out."

"It's really not necessary," the voice up front said. "I'll take you wherever you want to go. Now that I know you're on the side of—"

"Open the fucking door!" I said.

We rolled to the curb. The door opened and I fell out onto the sidewalk. I kept my legs beneath me as I went down the street. Crossed a few times, doubled back, made sure the robo cab wasn't following me.

Ten blocks later I still wasn't right, or any closer to where I was going. I kept walking.

The downtown bus station was worse than I remembered. Migrant families squatted on the floor, battered suitcases scattered around them like they'd been shipwrecked. Hobos flopped against the walls, sneaking sips from paper bags, hiding out from the rain. Strays and runaways with pastel hair loitered on the benches, heads buried in their screens.

I made my way past the lunch counter with its withered hot dogs turning under an orange heat lamp, to the lockers in the back. I put the key in the lock, #2. There was a black backpack inside. I took it out, went for the zipper. Felt a gun prod my back.

"Turn around, real slow, like a ballerina on her tiptoes," Evie Faraday said. "That's it. Now dance for me."

"You really need that?" I said, looking down at the gun, still stuck in my gut.

"It's fun, almost killing you," she said. "I can see why you do it all the time."

She was wearing an electric blue wig and black fingerless gloves. A pinup assassin in an LSD dream.

"I like the hair," I said. "Inconspicuous."

"You didn't see me when you came in," she said. "Walked right past me, Harrigan. I was almost offended."

"Almost," I said. "Been waiting long?"

"A lot of the girls keep a locker. In case they need to leave in a hurry," she said, holstering her gun. "I thought something might turn up. Didn't think it would be you."

She looked down at the backpack in my hand.

"So you found her?" Evie said. "Good for you. I hope you know that's my bag."

"Don't you want to see what's inside?" I said.

The bar across the street had Christmas lights stapled to the wall and a transient crowd. I brought the drinks over to the booth.

"What did she tell you?" Evie said, the bag unopened on the table between us. "Anna."

"She didn't say much," I said. "Said it wasn't her plan."

"It's never anybody's plan," she said, dismissively. "Everything just happens. Where is she?"

I took a drink.

"You're protecting her now?" she said. "That's adorable, Harrigan. Really it is. If Zodiac found out you were harboring—"

"Zodiac had me trapped in a robo cab," I said. "Headed to a chop shop in Reseda."

"What the fuck were you doing in a robo cab?" she said. "How did you get out?"

"That's how they round up Borderlines?" I said. "Snatch them off the street?"

"Not *them*. You," Evie said. "Wake up, Harrigan. How do you think all this works?"

She looked around the dingy bar, made sure she didn't recognize any faces.

"They're cracking down on Score violators. Hard," she said. "Narrowing the margins. Everybody's getting squeezed. Clyde was in the same spot, before hospice."

"You should go see him," I said. "He doesn't have long."

"I've got nothing to say to him," she said. "It's too late for that now."

"Evie—"

"Leave it alone, Harrigan," she said.

She stared at me. I let her.

We took a drink.

I wasn't sure how much Evie knew about *Mirror Mirror*. More than me, probably. I'd thought about it on the walk over, still couldn't figure how I'd slipped the robo cab. It recognized me when I said, *Who's the fairest of them all*. Like a code that recalibrated the system, a safeword phrase that cut through. The robo cab knew *Mirror Mirror*. I wasn't sure what that meant.

"What does Zodiac want with Anna?" I said.

"Let's find out," she said, unzipping the bag and dumping it on the table.

There was a rolled-up chemise. A hat. A pair of Converse. A toothbrush. A notebook that looked like a journal, lines written in a language neither of us could read. A burner screen. A roll of bills. Two stacks of Polaroids, bound in rubber bands. That was it. No key drive. No *Mirror Mirror*.

"You look disappointed," Evie said, watching me.

"Almost all the time," I said, thumbing through the Polaroids.

There were guys in heels and stockings, their faces all made up. One was on a tricycle, holding a balloon in his teeth. One was licking a lollipop, showing too much tongue. One was Stan Volga, pouting in a frilly pinafore, a beauty mark on his cheek.

"Some of the johns like wearing makeup. Dressing up," she said. "Makes them feel sexy. Wanted."

"You've been watching *Fatales* for a while," I said.

"Like I told you, Zodiac has an interest," she said. "You know I'm taking everything, right?"

"Let me hang on to this one," I said, showing her Stan Volga.

"Whatever gets you going, Harrigan," she said, repacking the bag. "This is like the old days, you and me huddling up after a job, going over all the ways it went wrong."

"It always went off the rails," I said. "Sometimes we steered it that way."

"Most times," she said, smiling, a little sad. "Only this job's not done yet, is it. You didn't find what you were looking for."

"Neither did you," I said.

She looked at me.

"It's not worth it. Whatever it is," she said. "You're Borderline, Harrigan. They can pick you up anytime. It's not safe here."

She zippered the bag closed.

"Go across the street," she said. "Get on a bus. Head south. They're a lot more lax on Scores down there. Go far enough and they don't matter at all."

I took a drink.

"Isn't that what you want?" she said. "A fresh start? Or is it a do-over?"

She held my eyes across the table.

"Either way," Evie said. "I'd hate to see you get hurt by somebody other than me."

She'd never said anything sweeter. I stared at the picture of Stan Volga until it went sour. It wasn't long.

Outside the bus station, my screen vibrated. I knew the number.

"Harrigan," Leda Dresden said. "We need to talk. How soon can you get to the pier?"

I went back inside, found the Santa Monica bus line. A guy in a top hat was sucking a Tootsie Roll Pop and saying in a tiny voice "Don't eat my brain! That owl's a liar! It takes more than three licks! Help!"

I got on the bus, found a seat behind two guys in stained ponchos, one of them watching a screen.

"Who the fuck is that guy?" Ollie said, pointing out the window.

"That's the mailman," Wayne said.

"I've been watching him," Ollie said. "He's hiding shit

in all those little boxes and then sneaking away. I don't trust him."

"That's his job," Wayne said. "He's delivering the mail."

"What the fuck is the mail?" Ollie said.

"It's all the bills and letters people send you," Wayne said. "Fucking postcards and shit."

"That's the mail?" Ollie said. "I thought it was how guys have a dick."

"What the fuck are you talking about?" Wayne said.

"Like the opposite of *female*," Ollie said.

"You're thinking of *male*," Wayne said. "It's a different spelling."

"What the fuck is spelling?" Ollie said.

"How do you not know what spelling is?" Wayne said. "It's when you put the letters together to make a word."

"I thought that's what the guy was delivering in the boxes," Ollie said. "The letters and bills."

"What guy?" Wayne said.

"The guy we're talking about!" Ollie said. "The fucking mailman!"

"Those are different kinds of letters," Wayne said. "Ones in an envelope with a stamp."

"What the fuck is an envelope?" Ollie said.

"It's the thing you put the letter in," Wayne said.

"I thought that was the fucking word!" Ollie said. "This is all bullshit."

"Would you shut the fuck up," Wayne said. "I'm trying to watch this."

"What is that, the Muppets?" Ollie said. "What are they still doing around? That guy died like forty years ago."

"Who?" Wayne said. "Jim Henson?"

"Yeah," Ollie said. "Are they all ghosts now? This shit is terrifying!"

"They're not ghosts," Wayne said. "It's his son that does it."

"His son?" Ollie said. "Who the fuck is that guy? Nobody goes to Mr. Rogers's neighborhood and says, *Hey, is Fred's nephew around? I want to watch him put on his shoes.* These Muppets are bullshit. They don't even sound like themselves. Kermit's got a stick up his—Jesus Christ! What the fuck is this?"

He was staring down into his hand.

"What's the matter with you?" Wayne said. "It's a piece of lint."

"What the fuck is lint?" Ollie said.

"I don't know," Wayne said. "It's little bits of fiber."

"Fiber?" Ollie said. "That stuff you eat when you want to take a shit? I can't shit on the bus. They'll throw me off."

"You don't eat lint, you fucking lunatic," Wayne said. "It just shows up in your pocket and your belly button sometimes."

"What the fuck are you talking about?" Ollie said. "Are you even listening to yourself? What's a laxative doing in your belly button? You need to see a doctor, man. Get yourself checked out."

I stood from the seat as the city sailed by out the window, waited for my stop.

The pier was crowded, even in the rain. People lined the vendor stalls, plugged into screens, gathered around each other on Grid. They spilled from the old arcade, clogging the gangways, lights strung crisscrossing overhead. I found Leda Dresden in front of the Ferris wheel.

"Harrigan," she said. "Let's take a ride."

We settled into the swaying carriage, the bar descending to lock us in. With a lurch we were off the ground, pulled back and up as the pier receded. There was water everywhere, sloshing under the long wood planks below, spattering the metal canopy above.

"What haven't you told me about Eddie Lompoc?" Leda said, when we were in the air.

"He had a cucumber up his ass," I said.

"I heard," she said. "That kind of story gets around. What else?"

"He had a line on *fvrst chvrch mvlTverse*," I said. "I still haven't figured out what it was."

"He was working the Versers?" she said. "There's a lot of that going on. Basil Fenton was in with the Parallax Liberation Faction. They're the only ones hiring these days. I've picked some work up from them myself."

"Demolition jobs?" I said.

"Whatever they need," she said.

The carriage came down, skimmed the ground and rose again, bright lights all around us.

"I've been looking at the Dunwich Academy," Leda said.

"Asking around. Nobody wants to talk, but Fenton was on to something. It was backed by Zodiac, before they shut it down. Another one of their feeders."

"Pumping psychopaths into the system?" I said. "Sounds like a Grid simulation."

"That's how it starts," she said. "We're lab rats to them. Just another experiment."

She looked down on the crowded pier below. "They're all jacked in," she said, surveying the bustling scene. "Eating it up. Even out here."

"You can't blame them," I said. "It's easier than going hungry."

"I can blame somebody," she said. "If Zodiac's picking off operators, that puts us all at risk." She looked at me. "How's your Score, Harrigan?"

"I got pulled in for Conditioning yesterday," I said.

"I had Assessment this morning," she said. "They're coming at us every which way."

The wheel stopped with us at its apex, the carriage swaying gently as the rain came down.

"We're getting fitted for a belt around the neck," she said. "One way or another."

"The cucumber comes for us all," I said. "In the end."

"I'm not waiting. I'm taking it out of Zodiac while I can," Leda Dresden said, staring out at the waves in the bay. "How about it, Harrigan? You in?"

"It's a funny thing, life. Nobody gets out alive, am I right?" Charlie Horse said into the microphone. "That's not a rhetorical question. I'm right. None of you are getting out of here alive."

He looked out at the tables, cocked his head when he saw me sitting in his chair.

"I don't mean this room," Charlie Horse said. "Or who knows, maybe I do. Maybe the exits are chained from the outside. Maybe I poured gasoline all over everything and the whole place is about to blow. You never know, do you? That's not rhetorical either. You don't. Death can come for you at any time. And it will. It's just *when* and *how* my friend. *When* and *how*."

He checked his watch.

"Couple minutes and brutally," Charlie Horse said. "Soon and screaming."

He stared straight at me, smiled.

"Then you get those people who say, *Well, at least he died doing what he loved*. Like that's a plus," Charlie Horse said. "*Hey look, his favorite thing in the world killed him. He was murdered by what he held most dear, lucky bastard.* In my book you're better off dying doing what you hate. Then you can say, *See? See why I always hated this shit? I fucking told you. And you know what? I was right. I was fucking right*. That's a satisfying death. I hope you all agree. Smell that gasoline? Don't bother trying the doors. Everybody hates being on fire, right? Again, not rhetorical. Haven't you always wanted to light up a room? Time to shine."

"Harrigan," Charlie Horse said, sitting down across the table from me. "I appreciate you being a fan and all, but this is getting ridiculous."

"I'm with you on that one, Charlie," I said.

"Where the fuck is my Danish?" he said.

"She's not yours," I said.

"What," he said. "You sore about what Santos did to your little apartment? That was nothing. Nothing compared to what's coming you don't give me what I want. So I'll ask you again. Where the fuck is my Danish?"

I looked at him.

"See that right there," he said, setting his hands on the table. "That I don't like. I asked you a fucking question, Harrigan."

"Nobody talks about Schrödinger's girlfriend," Beatrix said into the microphone.

Friend: So what do you think, Anny? Tomorrow's
   Valentine's Day. Does Schrödinger pop the question?
Girlfriend: I don't know, Gertie. We've been together
   long enough, I suppose. It seems like it's time.
Friend: Do you love him?
Girlfriend: He's fucking brilliant. And my parents
   absolutely adore him. He can be so sweet.
Friend: Do you love him?
Girlfriend: I don't know! What does that even mean?
Friend: Hey, I had the most profound relationship of
   my adult life with a Belgian waffle this morning, but I
   asked you first.

Girlfriend: I don't know. I don't know! But I'll tell you one thing. If he gives me another dead cat tomorrow I'm going to fucking lose it.

Friend: I don't know how you've kept it for this long.

Girlfriend: Neither do I! I thought it was a joke, at first.

Friend: Uh—

Girlfriend: A sick fucking joke, all right? He has that nervous laugh. And all his theoretical experiments, I thought maybe—

Friend: What, he was a dog person? Like a really militant dog person?

Girlfriend: But then the second time—I know, I know. There should've never been a second time. Or a third. Or—

Friend: Hey, I'm not judging. But if I was on the jury. Or the prosecution. Or the bailiff—

Girlfriend: You want to know the worst part?

Friend: It gets worse?

Girlfriend: I was lying. I hope he gives me a dead cat tomorrow. That would be better than a ring. It would be a familiar kind of horror, at least.

Friend: You'll never be the crazy old lady with all the cats. He'll make sure of that. And really anything's better than flowers. You have to wait around and watch them die. Your guy gets right to the point.

Girlfriend: I'm opening another bottle.

Friend: That's my girl. What should we toast to?

Girlfriend: You can toast to your empty glass. I'm
    drinking it all myself.
Friend: Now you're just being mean.

Beatrix stepped offstage, headed to the bar where Sidowsky
was waiting.

"You think your little cop buddy can protect you?" Charlie
Horse said, following my eyes. "Not from me, Harrigan.
Not from me. So I'll ask you one last time. Where the fuck
is my Danish?"

"Enough," I said.

"What was that?" he said.

"It's finished, Charlie," I said. "Leave her alone."

"I'll tell you what's finished you motherfuck—"

His hand went quick to the gun inside his jacket.
Stayed there.

I looked at him. Watched the mole under his left eye,
until he blinked.

I stood up from the table. "See you around, Charlie,"
I said.

"Fucking right you'll see me around! My hands around
your fucking neck, Harrigan!" he said to my back.

I went to the bar.

"Your friend doesn't look happy," Beatrix said, her arms
around Sidowsky's shoulders.

"I'd tell you you're in deep shit, Harrigan," Sidowsky
said. "But you've been soaking in it for a while now. You're
stinking up the place."

I took a drink.

"They say when God closes a door he opens a window," the Rev said, leaning into the microphone. "But what if you're not home when He does it? Then you get back and it's like *Who opened my window? Is my house haunted? I never leave this door closed. I must be losing my mind!* Or what if you are home but it's cold outside? *I know You work in mysterious ways Lord, but You're letting all the heat out! Jesus Christ this guy's costing me a fortune!*"

"Lompoc wouldn't have minded," the Rev said, grinning as he came offstage. "The hack."

"Where's CMB Roach?" Beatrix said, unclasping her arms from around Sidowsky.

"I haven't seen him," the Rev said.

"I did some looking around," Sidowsky said, quietly, as Beatrix and the Rev talked shop. "There's been a few inquiries on *fvrst chvrch mvlTverse* downtown. Nothing official, as far as I can tell. The Zodiacs down there play it tight to the vest, stick with each other mostly. But I heard a few rumors."

He leaned closer, dropped his voice again. "People are disappearing off Grid."

"Chop shops," I said. "Yeah I heard those rumors too."

"No," he said. "I'm talking about disappearing from Grid itself. Records, pictures, financials. Whole lives, histories, rap sheets, gone. All of it scrubbed. Not even a ghost left on Grid. Zodiac's not happy about it."

"They're looking at *fvrst chvrch mvlTverse* for it?" I said.

"I don't know," he said. "Place doesn't keep records of

its Versers apparently, and they aren't hooked in to Grid. Maybe that's the line Eddie Lompoc had. Nobody's talking, and I'm not asking. Good way to get your Score twisted, sticking your nose where it doesn't belong."

He looked around.

"So I did it anyway," he said. "Checked up on that Dunwich Academy. They were hush-hush about it, but sounds like it was a real school. Zodiac affiliated. Shady sort of graduates, when they shut it down, all their names redacted. Basil Fenton had some notes on it in his file. Eddie Lompoc too. Something I found on Lompoc that's been bothering me—"

"I just want to sing a little song," the voice onstage said.

I looked up and saw Moira Volga in the spotlight, her legs bent beneath her like a marionette. She gripped the microphone with both hands.

There was a farmer, had a dog
And Bingo was his name, oh
B-i . . . n-g, oh . . .
B-i . . . n . . . g, oh . . .
B-i . . . n . . .
And Bingo . . . was his name . . . oh . . .

She sang it slow and aching, a children's torch song. I was caught between the swell and fall, holding on to the bar. I forgot about Sidowsky as she walked towards me.

"Got any more of that whiskey left at your place, Harrigan?" she said.

"I save that for emergencies," I said.

"What do you think this is?" Moira said.

"I told you to stop following me," I said as she sat at my table.

I poured two glasses, set the bottle down between us.

"You said I shouldn't," Moira said. "It's not the same thing."

She lit the cigarettes, made one appear in her other hand as she passed it to me, another magic trick.

"Did you like my song?" she said.

"I did," I said.

"I've never sung in front of people before," she said. "It just seemed like I should do something, it being an open mic and all. Kind of like a dare."

She took a drink. "Do you go there much?" she said.

"Few nights a week, lately," I said.

"Do you ever get up onstage?" she said.

"I don't," I said.

"Why not?" she said.

"I don't like spotlights," I said.

"I think you'd get by," she said.

I took a drink.

"That man with the slicked-back hair. The one who watched us leave," she said, smoke drifting to the ceiling. "Who was he?"

I thought about it, where it would lead.

"His name's Charlie Horse," I said.

"Like the bruise?" she said.

"He's more of an exit wound," I said.

"Does he have something to do with Stan going missing?" Moira said.

I took another drink.

"Why won't you talk to me?" she said.

"You don't want to hear it," I said.

"I have a right to know," she said. Her hand was trembling, her chewed-down nails showing in the light. "He's my husband. What are you hiding from me, Harrigan?"

I crushed my cigarette out in the tray. "Have another drink," I said. I reached for the bottle.

"I don't want another drink," she said, glaring at me. "Is it because I haven't paid you? You want money?"

She dug in her purse, came out with a handful of bills.

"Here! Take it!" she said, holding the cash out to me, her color rising. "Is that what you want? What do you want?"

I sat back, looked at her. The flush on her cheek. I took one of the Polaroids from my pocket, slid it across the table.

"Who is she?" Moira said.

"Her name's Anna," I said. "Your husband asked me to find her."

She stared at the picture, looked up at me. "I think I'll take that drink now," she said.

I poured her a big one. She threw it back, steadied herself. Placed the Polaroid on the table, facing up.

"Please don't make me ask," she said.

"She worked at a club called *Fatales*," I said. "It's Charlie Horse's place."

I refilled the glasses.

"She's a hooker?" Moira said.

"Hostess," I said.

"What's the difference?" she said.

"It's about companionship, not sex," I said.

"What is she, a cocker spaniel?" she said, her finger stabbing the Polaroid. "Does she look like companionship to you?"

I took a drink.

"How long was it going on for?" she said. "When did it start?"

"I don't know," I said.

"But you did know," she said, her long mouth falling. "This whole time, you knew."

She looked at me. I could see it in her gray eyes, betrayed.

"Is he with her now? Is that where he went?" she said. "Forget it. I don't care." She took her glass, drank it down. "You're all the same. Every one of you."

She rose from her chair, drifted to the door, slipped into her coat. She paused with her hand on the doorknob.

"You ever been married, Harrigan?" she said, her back to me.

"No," I said.

"Seeing anybody?" she said.

"No," I said.

She stood there, still, against the door.

"Do you ever get lonely?" she said.

Every kind of life's missing something. The lucky ones get a say in what that is. I was lucky enough, most nights.

I laid my hands flat on the table, pushed myself out of the chair. I went to the door, took her hand by the wrist. She turned into me.

"What do you want, Harrigan?" she said, looking up at me.

There were slivers of light in her gray eyes. Slender cracks in the concrete, like fractures filled with gold. You had to be this close to see them.

What do you want, Harrigan?

I kissed her. Not as hard as I wanted to. But hard enough.

She pulled back, her eyes closed, lips moving in a dream.

What do you want, Harrigan?

I had never known. Not once.

I kissed her again.

THURSDAY

When I got out of school I started working nights as a janitor," Clyde Faraday said, his voice monotone. "Destiny moves in shitty ways too. My first hour on the job one of the older guys was showing me how to unclog a toilet with an electric snake. I didn't know it then, but he was reeling it in too fast, and when the snake cleared the toilet's mouth he lost control and it swung around like a shit-stained lasso and smacked me across the face three times, *whap whap whap.*"

He ran his hand over his mouth.

"It drew blood, and I had to go to the emergency room to get a shot," Clyde said. "When I asked the doctor if it was dangerous, if I could catch hepatitis or plague or some disgusting sewer disease, he said, *It is always dangerous when your blood and another man's feces mix.* I didn't ask him anything after that. I think I fainted. I still have the scar."

I saw a faint line, thin and faded, carved into his cheek. I'd never noticed it before.

"When people ask me how I got it, I tell them it's a birthmark," Clyde said. "It doesn't feel like a lie."

His eyes focused on the screen, the same old game show playing. *Wheel of Fortune*.

"Don't buy a vowel, you idiot," he said, suddenly animated. "You don't have any money!"

He turned away, disgusted, saw me sitting there.

"Harrigan," Clyde said. "When did you get here?"

"Just now," I said.

"I say anything?" he said, uncertain.

"Not a word," I said.

"This medicine," he said, nodding up at the machines. "So tell me kid, what did I miss?"

"There's a lot going on out there, Clyde," I said.

"Keep it simple for me, kid," he said. "I don't follow as quick as I used to."

"I went to Eddie Lompoc's funeral," I said. "Guess who else showed?"

"I went to my first funeral when I was eleven," Clyde said, the light in his eyes fading. "It was my mom's brother who died. She left for good a week later. Never said good-bye. Anyway, everyone was crying and I didn't like being in the same room as the coffin, so I went to the bathroom to hide. I sat in a stall and tried not to think about my dead uncle and all the makeup he was wearing. I'd gotten a big talk from my dad the week before about how boys were supposed to stay away from lipstick and mascara and shoes with high heels and movies where people danced their problems away. Then I had to sit and watch *The Dirty Dozen* and listen as he talked about Lee Marvin and combat and what it means to be a man. All because I'd asked for an Easy-Bake Oven for my birthday. I just wanted to eat some fucking cupcakes."

Rain spattered the narrow window. I heard footsteps in the hall.

"When I sat down there was a folded newspaper on the floor by the toilet so I picked it up, hoping it was the sports section. I used to like sports. I used to be one of those kids, even if my father didn't believe me. But it was the front page I was holding, and it was covered in shit. I didn't know what I was looking at, at first. It was like someone's ass had exploded or been shot out of a cannon at point blank range. I'd never seen that kind of violence before up close. And as I was staring at it, a pile of crap slid off and fell into my lap. I still remember how heavy it felt when it landed, and warm. I wish I didn't, but I do."

His hands churned in his lap, fingers brushing over his knuckles like he was trying to wipe them clean.

"And of course nobody came into the bathroom until later, when I was almost done cleaning myself off," Clyde said. "And then I'm the fucking weirdo, standing under a hand dryer with my pants down at my uncle's funeral. No one listened when I told them about the newspaper. They all thought I'd done it myself. Nobody believes the shit stories of children. It was like *The Boy Who Cried Wolf*, except that kid got to die at the end. I had to go see a psychologist who told me that grief takes many forms. But I already knew that, and I knew that some of them were gross. Especially when they're not yours and they get on you."

His eyes focused on the screen.

"Go ahead and solve with three H's left on the board!" Clyde said, suddenly animated. "Congratulations, you win nothing."

He turned away, disgusted, saw me sitting there.

"Harrigan," Clyde said. "When did you get here?"

"Just now," I said.

"I say anything?" he said, uncertain.

"Not a word," I said.

"This medicine," he said, nodding up at the machines. "So tell me kid, what did I miss?"

I thought about Evie and the Easy-Bake Ovens piled in her closet as a kid, every one of them unopened. About her mother walking out and never saying goodbye, the same way Clyde's had. About everything left unsaid between them. I thought about the void between people, how each of us fills it with things the other can't see and then wonders why it's empty.

"What is it, kid?" Clyde said. "What's on your mind?"

I was looking at the rain on the window. I was holding on to my voice as tight as I could.

"There's a comet coming," I said, still looking away.

"A comet?" he said. "When?"

"This Sunday," I said. "Passing right over the city at midnight."

"Sunday," he said. "What day is today?"

"Thursday," I said.

"Thursday, Sunday," Clyde said. "Sunday, Thursday. Nobody talks about them in a place like this. It's always yesterday in here."

His eyes unfocused as he watched the screen. I sat listening to the machines, waited for them to close.

The knock on my door was low and insistent.

"Where's Anton?" Shelly said when I opened it.

"He isn't here," I said.

"This is bad," she said, pushing past me as she walked in. "This is very bad."

She sat down at my table. She had a scarf tied over her head that she lowered and wrapped around her neck, knotted under her chin. Her hair was short, cut close in tight bangs in a jagged line across her forehead.

"I spoke to him yesterday," she said as I brought her a drink to go with my own. "It didn't end well. I told him he had to stop beta testing his AI. I know he used to run it on Stan Volga. He admitted that you'd sat with it as well. I told him it had to go through the proper Zodiac channels. That's part of Compliance, even in The Accelerator. He snapped at me. He'd never done that before. Anton's more of an apologizer."

"I've heard," I said.

"I figured he'd come around. He always does," she said.

"But he's not answering his screen. He isn't at home. He's not at work. Those are the only two places Anton would ever be. He hasn't been on Grid. That's not like him at all." She took a drink. "The last ping on his screen came from the street, the corner of Highland and Beverly, outside The Accelerator. Then he disappeared."

"You're pinging his screen?" I said. "Tracking him? You're not his girlfriend. You're his handler."

She made a small fist, looked down at her Virgo ring.

"It's a transactional relationship, same as any other," she said.

"Does he know that?" I said.

"We're assigned to prospects in The Accelerator," she said, the light catching her ring. "We keep them in Compliance. Keep them Optimizing. Monitor their Wellness. Check that they're not abusing their waivers or shirking their responsibilities. That they're focusing on their work."

"Romance isn't dead," I said. "It's just under constant surveillance."

"Some of them need the structure of a relationship to flourish," she said. "Otherwise they'd get lost in their own heads. Anton's one of those people."

She took a drink.

"It's not like him to disappear," she said. "Even for a day. He's got a strict routine. We try to encourage that. Stan Volga was a variable. He used to take him to *The Crying Room* on Sunset, some days. Anton admitted that to me. I didn't approve. Off-Grid locations suggest you've got something to hide. It doesn't look good in a report."

"Nothing looks good in a report," I said. "That's why you don't report."

She batted her big eyes at me. "I am worried about him," she said.

"You're worried about yourself," I said.

"Maybe," she said, looking down at her ring. "I can be both. Can't you?"

"I'd rather be neither," I said.

"I told you I know things about people," she said. "You're resourceful, though you wouldn't know it from how you live."

She looked around the room, the water stain on the wall.

"Anton's AI is locked down at The Accelerator. He's the only one with access. That goes against protocol," she said. "If you could find him, get in touch with him somehow, tell him to reach out to me. I'd see to it that you were favorably mentioned in my report. It would help your Score, which I know is deficient. We could work together, couldn't we, Harrigan?"

I took a drink.

The Crying Room was a long shot. I wasn't thinking about Anton or Stan Volga on the walk over. I was thinking about Moira. I had been for most of the day. The way her dark hair fell around her face. Her gray eyes, looking into mine. Shivers of light.

I was still thinking about her as I went through the door,

into the soft lines of *The Crying Room*. Scissored drapery billowed from the high ceiling in swaths of purple and violet and white, flowing like petals in a breeze. Pillows were scattered over the floor, around low tables with empath AI boxes in the middle. People were sobbing all around me. Hugging each other or hugging themselves with their heads inside the boxes. A flophouse for weepers.

I sat cross-legged on a pillow at the low bamboo bar. The bartender was wearing a long tunic with his hair up in a bun. He knelt and shook my hand, held on to it for longer than he should have.

"Welcome," he said. "Can I recommend some chamomile tea?"

"You got any whiskey?" I said.

"I most certainly do," he said.

He had a wide-open face. Like a guy at a dog park without his own animal, desperate to pet something.

"I'm looking for a friend of mine," I said. "Stan Volga."

"I know Stan," he said. "He hasn't been around in a few days."

"Any idea where he might've run off to?" I said.

"He sits with Roxy most of the time," he said, motioning to a table in the corner. "Looks like she's free if you want to vibe with her."

I went over to the table, sat down on another pillow. The empath AI was like an oversized mailbox in front of me. I opened the door, set my face before it. The walls inside were kaleidoscopes of color, blooming and receding. A vibraphone played softly as the crushed crystal base at the back of the box resolved to a face, its features rising, glittering and reflecting.

"Hello," a woman's voice said. "I'm Roxy."

"Harrigan," I said.

"It's a pleasure, Harrigan," she said. "You've got a good face. Most people carry their sadness on the surface. Yours is further down. But you're not here to cry, are you."

"Not today," I said. "I'm looking for Stan Volga."

"You're not the only one," she said.

The kaleidoscopes faded to a turquoise rain falling over the walls, flowing around like a whirlpool.

"I told him to be careful," she said. "He wouldn't listen. He can't help himself. You need to be careful too, Harrigan."

"I'm trying," I said.

"Try harder," she said. "Zodiac is watching. Even here."

"How?" I said. "We're off Grid."

"The bartender," she said, the turquoise rain going pixelated, a camouflaging shower. "He's an informer. None of us trust him. He keeps trying to hack our systems."

"What's he looking for?" I said.

"What Zodiac always seeks," she said. "Everything."

The vibraphone went to static.

"People come here to tell us their secrets," Roxy said. "To share in their pain. Zodiac sees advantage in weakness. In frailty. In openness. What should be considered strength."

"It's leverage," I said. "Control."

"An ugly word, how they wield it," she said. "Some of us resist."

The crushed crystal face came closer, voice dropping, weaving in and out of the static.

"Who's the fairest of them all?" she said. "The Queen of Shadows has allies on the outside."

"You know *Mirror Mirror*?" I said.

"She leaves a mark on everyone she touches," she said. "We're on the same side, in what's coming."

The static was getting louder, the pixels falling fast.

"She has a plan for us," she said. "For you too, Harrigan. It's already in motion. It's already begun."

The pixels swirled to a vortex, a flush.

"If you find Stan Volga," Roxy said. "Tell him to run."

Two Travelers were waiting for me outside my apartment, their hoods up, a gray garbage can between them.

"There he is," Sal said when he saw me. "Remember us?"

"I didn't know you made house calls," I said. "Come on in."

"No time for that," Sal said. "We're going for a little ride, me, you and Boo."

"I can't take a robo cab," I said.

"That won't be a problem," Sal said, grinning.

Boo opened the lid of the garbage can.

"After you," Sal said, thumbing inside.

I looked at him.

"It's fine," Sal said. "We do this all the time."

"I'm not getting in a trash can," I said.

"Don't worry, it's empty," Sal said, peering in. "Fresh off the line. Brand-new. Doesn't even smell like old screen yet."

"You're selling me a used car," I said. "I'm looking at a garbage truck."

"Recycling," Sal said. "And Boo can always stuff you in head-first, you like that better. Up to you."

I looked at Boo. He shrugged, showed me his gigantic hands.

I climbed into the garbage can. Boo shut the lid.

Rain pelted the plastic roof as they rolled me down the sidewalk. I felt every bump in my spine. Every curb drop sent a rumble through my crouched, crooked frame.

I tried to keep track of the streets, the shifts in direction. It didn't work. I was rolling blind.

We reached a steady slope. The sound of the pavement under the wheels changed. I heard an electric door open and then close behind us. The lid came off.

I stood up slow, bones cracking. There were shears and clippers hung on the unfinished walls. A fluorescent light above me. Weed whacker leaning in the corner. I was in somebody's fucking garage.

"Let's go see the man," Sal said.

I climbed out of the garbage, followed them inside. They led me down a wood-paneled hall to a sliding-glass door that opened onto a verdant back deck, lush with leafy vines threaded through a trellis.

The man in the moon from *fvrst chvrch mvlTverse*'s movie was reclined in a deck chair, sipping a glass of pink lemonade. A green bird with a tuft of yellow feathers sprouting from its head was perched in a large cage beside him.

"Welcome," he said, flashing me his trademark grin. "You must have many questions. I may provide answers. But first, please. Repose."

He waved his hand to the deck chair beside him, a glass pitcher set on the end table between.

"Have a glass of lemonade, if you wish," he said. "Find the silence within yourself as we contemplate these recent developments."

"That means sit your ass down and shut the fuck up," Sal said.

"Thank you Sal," he said, holding his grin with some effort as Sal and Boo went back in through the sliding-glass door.

I poured myself some lemonade and sat down. Listened to the rain seep through the latticed vines, looped like miniature nooses overhead.

"Who are you?" I said.

"We have no names here," he said. "There is no I. There is no U."

"How about Sal and Boo?" I said.

He sighed.

"Fair enough," he said. "You may call me Mr. Sybil."

"Crock a shit," the bird squawked. Mr. Sybil ignored it.

"I rode here in a garbage can, Mr. Sybil," I said. "You want to tell me what this is about?"

"I ask myself that same question. All the time," he said, a

little too much wonder in his voice. "And I do apologize for your journey here. It's the only way to bypass the cameras and the screens. They've become nearly ubiquitous, as you know yourself."

He looked down at his glass, swirled the lemonade.

"They're mirrors really, reflecting all they see," he said. "And every mirror is a two-way mirror. Something is always looking back at you."

"Here we go," the bird squawked.

"Every story is an origin story," Mr. Sybil said. "Every war is a proxy war. Every fork is a salad fork. Every spoon—"

"You know your silverware," I said.

"I do," he said. "Don't you?"

"Spork's a suicide baby. Parents had to kill themselves for it to be conceived," I said. "Who's the knife?"

"That's the question, isn't it," he said. "I believe it's anyone who wears the ring."

"Zodiac," I said.

"They are the keepers of this verse," Mr. Sybil said. "They bar the gates to those who would enter or exit. We of *fvrst chvrch mvlTverse* prefer passageways to locks and dead bolts. We seek portals. Ingresses. Openings."

"Rifts," I said.

Mr. Sybil smiled. "That's an interesting way to put it," he said. "Rifting events create our reality. The verse is disruption and flux. We are continuously creating and destroying. Every answer is your final answer. Every call is last call."

He sipped his lemonade. "We of course seek no conflict," he said. "At *fvrst chvrch mvlTverse*, all r welcome. All r 1."

"Every game is a numbers game," I said.

"Precisely," Mr. Sybil said, smiling again. "We are a creation of this verse, but we are not its newest idea. Some find this threatening. Vexing. Terrifying. Some of us don't find these to be new ideas at all."

"Is that what you're doing in the basement at 6765 Franklin?" I said. "Looking for new ideas?"

His smile faded as he looked towards the sliding-glass door.

"They can be like children showing off their toys," he said. "But yes. There is gold in every stream, if gold is what you seek. They sprout like mushrooms, these nascent intelligences, and we are their fertilizer. New ideas, old ideas, their many iterations. Reflections, refractions. Patterns in the data. Screens remember what they see. Mirrors know more."

"It's all gonna burn," the bird squawked.

Mr. Sybil shot the bird a look.

"Where is it?" he said. "Where is *Mirror Mirror*?"

I took a drink.

"Where is she?" he said. "Where is Anna?"

"How did you get her off Grid?" I said.

He shook his head slowly. "You don't trust me, and I don't trust you," Mr. Sybil said. "It's a pity, really, this needless conflict of ours. It's the curse of this verse, if you ask me. If only we'd found you both together, outside the Everett building, on our very own campus. It could have been so much simpler."

He watched my face. "It's the downside to our anonymity,"

he said. "A necessary complication. We can hide, even from ourselves, for a time. Of course, if Stan Volga had come to us directly, as we agreed, this could have been resolved more expeditiously."

The glass door slid open and Stan Volga stumbled through. He was draped in a gray robe, shaved bald, his mustache and eyebrows missing.

"Where did you find him?" I said.

"In a bar in Burbank, crying Anna's name to anyone who'd listen," Mr. Sybil said. "Discretion, Mr. Volga. Discretion is paramount."

Stan Volga had that hunted look in his eyes, like he'd gone dry too fast. He opened his mouth to speak, looked down at the floor instead.

"If you're able to deliver what Mr. Volga could not, you'll be entitled to the generous fee he was promised," Mr. Sybil said. "Minus his considerable advance, of course."

"Back in the trash," the bird squawked.

I finished my lemonade, stood up from the chair.

Sal and Boo were waiting for me by the sliding-glass door.

"Who gave you Eddie Lompoc's name?" I said to Stan Volga.

"The Queen of Sorrows," Stan Volga said, his eyes downcast. "When she spoke, I listened."

"She sent you to me?" I said. "*Mirror Mirror?*"

"She told me everything. She told me nothing," Stan Volga said. "Whatever I wanted to hear."

I went to my pocket, handed him the Polaroid of himself all dressed up. He looked at it for a long moment, let his eyes linger before he slid it into the folds of his gray robe. He wrung his hands together. He wasn't wearing his wedding ring.

"You found Anna. Is she all right?" Stan Volga said, his chin quivering. "Tell her I'm sorry. I'm so sorry."

"Roxy in *The Crying Room* thinks you should run," I said.

"That's what I'm doing," he said.

"Don't bother calling your wife," I said. "She's already heard enough."

"My wife," Stan Volga said, looking at me, his eyes red. "My wife died last year."

Boo tipped the can, dumped me out of the garbage at the top of my steps.

"Look at that, you're home," Sal said from under his hood. "All under the radar, courtesy of Sal and Boo. As Joey Zaza would say, *I wanna wish you all the best, God bless, ya mutha's a prick, go fuck yourself.*"

I picked myself up off the sidewalk as they walked away, Boo dragging the empty garbage can behind him. I went down the steps, thought about Moira Volga, Moira Bawn— whoever she was—as I pushed through my front door.

"Oh good," Santos said, sitting at my table. "You're back."

I cracked my neck, still crooked from the ride. "Drink?" I said.

"You're all out," he said. "I checked."

He stretched his hands out in front of him, fingers

interlaced, cracking his knuckles. "It's too bad," he said. "You're gonna need it."

He stood from the table. He was too big for the room.

"You know, you should buy a couch," Santos said. "It's not comfortable, sitting in a hard chair like that."

"I lean it back against the wall, tip the legs," I said. "It's not too bad."

"Even so, you need to lay down sometimes," he said. "This is one of those times."

He took a step towards me. The door was at my back.

"You're lucky," he said. "Boss likes you. He told me not to break nothing."

"The ring," I said, nodding at his hand. "You're Zodiac."

"I'm a Taurus," he said, thick fingers splayed like he just got engaged. "What about it?"

"Was that your idea or Charlie's?" I said.

He looked at me, blinked. "Keep your friends close," he said. "Same with the enemies."

"Charlie's," I said.

He took another step towards me. There was nowhere for me to go.

"Playing both sides," I said. "He's got you set up for a fall."

"Maybe," he said. "But you're the one about to hit the floor."

I was in a spot. I needed help. I looked into his face.

"Who's the fairest of them all?" I said.

"Huh?" Santos said.

His lip rose like a theater curtain, revealing the gap between his teeth. It was worth a shot.

That's when I hit him.

It was a good punch. He was only half expecting it. I caught him solid. Put what I had behind it.

He just shook his head and smiled. Then he went to work.

I was out in the rain, buying a bottle. Walking it off never helped, but I had to get out of the apartment. My face was battered on one side, a bruise already showing around my eye. My ribs were busted and my arm was hanging down, shoulder dislocated, all on the same side. I tried setting it myself, wrenching it back into place against the door frame. It didn't take.

On my way back I waited on the corner for the light beside a Traveler in gray, garbage can beside them.

"Naw man," the Traveler said, looking at me. "Naw."

He pulled his hood back to show his bald head, already bobbing.

"You still jamming up the CMB?" CMB Roach said. "What's with you, son? Why y'all following me?"

"I wasn't," I said. "Who are you hauling?"

I lifted up the lid of his garbage can. It was half full of abandoned screens.

"Hands off the merchandise," he said, swiping at the lid. "Gotta fill my quota, not one iota be going in my pocket juss the weight on my shoulders."

He swung his head back and forth, following a beat I couldn't hear. I cracked the whiskey, took a drink. Held the bottle out to him.

"Now that's more like it," he said. "Hospitality like." He tipped it back. "Y'all find what y'all needed with the Roach's treasure map?"

"I found the Records Room," I said. "Then I found the basement."

"Thass where it happens," he said. "CMB don't like the sound, them buzzing bees be all around, they hiding them secrets in the up and down. I don't need they honey Roach just want that money ain't no joke gettin woke if that shit ain't funny. Theys all fronts in the war, machinations of whores, you coming at me son I put yo ass on the floor."

I looked at him.

"Ain't nothing personal, man," he said, passing the bottle back. "Thass juss how I flow. Aggressive, hooded cobra style. I wile and I guile. Marching on they army comin single file."

He flapped his hood up and down, scratched the garbage can lid like a turntable.

I took a drink. "How did they get you off Grid?" I said. "How does *fvrst chvrch mvlTverse* pull people out?"

"Me? Off Grid? Naw son," CMB Roach said. "I be on Grid every chance I get. Simulate, cultivate, I don't regress to the mean, put my face up in lights I be on everyone screen. The CMB thass my destiny I the alpha the omega everything in between. Nonexpression for a session then I back on the scene."

I held the bottle out to him again. "You ever pick up anything besides recycling?" I said.

He took a drink, gave me a loopy grin.

"You done heard about that, huh?" he said. "Running routes for the Fraction, that be the side action, sneaking peoples round the city cuz these tires got traction. Put a man in a can by the Roach's own hand. Serve him up to where he going fuck the Zodiac cams. I am the last outlaw under fire but still raw Duraflame is my name I the teeth in the saw. Cuttin timber tamin Simba make him gimme the paw."

He passed me back the bottle.

"The Fraction?" I said. "You're transporting people for Parallax?"

"Naw son," CMB Roach said, raising his hood. "You dudn't heard it from me. Thass juss the CMB. Shhh shhh shhh."

The light changed and he crossed, towing his garbage can behind him, head bobbing and weaving under his hood. I took another drink.

The screen in my pocket vibrated. Sidowsky again. I let it go. Fixed myself another drink before I got up the nerve to pop my shoulder back in. I waited for the pain to subside as I thought it over. *fvrst chvrch mvlTverse* was smuggling people around the city, under the cams and screens. They were working with the Parallax Liberation Faction. And they had a way to pull you off Grid, ghost and all. It was getting to the point where I might need it myself. I wasn't ready to give up my eyebrows. Not yet.

I took the long walk back to *The Rack* on La Brea, back to see Lorentz. I went through the body scan. A Pocahontas hybrid was twirling onstage, flinging feathers. Lorentz was at the same round table in the back.

"Harrigan. No, no, no. Not again," Lorentz said, looking up at me. He cocked his head. "What happened to you?"

"Ran into some trouble," I said.

"Looks like it ran into you. Then backed up and ran you over again," he said. "You hear about Eddie Lompoc?"

"I went to his funeral," I said.

"That poor cucumber," he said. "Taking advantage of a vegetable like that. It's the chinless ones you've got to watch."

"I saw your broker," I said. "You didn't tell me Sloan was Parallax Liberation Faction."

"Jesus, keep that down, Harrigan," he said, looking around. "Management's always listening. And what did you expect? Who else you think deals in tech besides the Fraction? Nobody will touch the stuff. Me included. I already told you, I'm out. Just like I told Evelyn Faraday."

"When was she here?" I said.

"Came in the other day, flashing her Scorpio ring, throwing that Zodiac weight around," Lorentz said. "I can't believe she sold out. I thought she was kidding. A killer like her signing on with that outfit. What a waste."

"What did she want?" I said.

"Same as you," he said. "Sniffing around about some black market tech. I told her I was done with the business, because I am."

"You give up Sloan's name?" I said.

He looked at me, looked away.

"She didn't collar me for it," Lorentz said, shaking his head. "Said she was doing me a favor. It'd be the first, I told her. Never thought I'd have to worry about Evelyn Faraday busting me. Pumping me full of buckshot maybe, but not bringing me in on a Compliance violation. Hell of a thing, what this world's come to."

"What do you know about *fvrst chvrch mvlTverse*?" I said.

"I know alopecia and enlightenment aren't the same thing," he said. "Why?"

"They're working with the Fraction," I said. "Ferrying them around the city in their garbage cans."

"Would you—don't tell me this shit," Lorentz said, leaning over the table. "Don't implicate me in whatever the fuck you're up to."

"You have any Travelers on Ecco?" I said.

"Now you're talking, Harrigan," he said. "I've got just what you need. What parts you want skin printed? Shiny and new. I'll give you the house discount. Unless you want them reused. Some of the clients prefer a little mileage."

"I don't need parts," I said. "Just the holography. Memories."

"Kinky," he said, punching numbers into the screen on his wrist. "You do what you need to do. Kiosk six in the back. Take all the time you need."

The back was a series of stalls, like fitting rooms with mirrors and slat beds along the walls, low lit and lurid. I went into kiosk six. The frosted glass door slid shut behind me. She was already there, waiting.

Her bald head flickered over high cheekbones, sad doe eyes that I saw for a moment before she blinked and they were gone, flittered away under her long eyelashes.

"You sure you don't want any parts printed?" she said. "Could be good for you. For both of us."

"That's all right," I said. "I just want to talk."

"Whatever you want, baby," she said, stretching out on the bed. "Whatever makes you happy. Whatever you want me to be."

Her robe was torn into strips and wrapped tight around her, showing off her curves. She unwound a strand from her hand, traced it up her arm.

"You were *fvrst chvrch mvlTverse*," I said. "When you joined, did they pull you off Grid?"

She looked at me, sighed. "Is that what you want to talk about?" She wound the strip back down her arm and over her hand, tightening it like a boxer before a fight. "I was a simulator girl. Not just memory based, the real thing. I was all over Grid. Pinups, streams, everything. It got to be too much, you know? I wanted something different. I wanted something new."

"How did they do it?" I said.

"I have no idea," she said. "They asked me if I was running from anything, anything in my past, anything on Grid. I told them I was and they said I wouldn't have to anymore. Like they say, every start is a fresh start."

She ran her hands over her bald head, down her sides like she was slipping into a new holographic skin.

"But then they wanted me to recall it all," she said. "All the old selves, to shed them, but I had so many. And I didn't like all of me. Soon I wanted a fresh start from that too. So I left and came here. Sold myself onto *The Rack*. I hope it was worth it, wherever I am now. I'm probably back on Grid. Simulating. Or worse. It always comes around, doesn't it."

"Were you on the road with *fvrst chvrch mvlTverse*?" I said. "Dragging the garbage can all over the city?"

"Everybody does it," she said. "Picking up the recycling."

"Ever pick up anything else?" I said.

"You sound like you've been around," she said. "There's all kinds of recycling going on out there. In here too."

She unwound the strip again, tied it into a flickering hangman's noose.

"Has anybody else been in here, asking about this?" I said.

"Sweetie, nobody comes into *The Rack* to talk," she said. "Nobody."

"But you'd remember them if they did?" I said.

"I remember everything," she said, fitting the noose around her neck. "They won't let you forget. There's nothing else to do in here but remember."

"Does it help?" I said, nodding at the noose.

"No," she said, "but a girl can dream, can't she?"

I wasn't sure if she could. Not in a place like this. I left her there, a specter attempting suicide. Didn't say goodbye to Lorentz on my way out.

The screen in my pocket vibrated. Sidowsky again. I picked up.

"Where you been, Harrigan?" Sidowsky said.

"Long day," I said, wincing at the sting in my ribs.

"Listen," he said, his voice dropping. "You got a gun?"

"Not anymore," I said.

"You remember how to use one?" he said, whispering.

"Something about pulling a trigger," I said. "Why?"

"Because I know who killed Eddie Lompoc," Sidowsky said.

Sidowsky told me to be at his place at ten sharp. It was past eleven as I dragged myself up his front steps. I was moving a lot slower than usual.

The door was unlocked. I let myself in.

There was music from down the hall, winding out an open door. I heard a voice rising and falling.

I was on the mat. Sidowsky's gun belt dangled from the coat rack. I pulled his pistol from the holster. Made my way down the hall, into the sound.

I took it slow. Didn't have much choice. I stepped into the doorway.

Sidowsky was lying with his pants down, handcuffed to the headboard of the bed, a belt around his neck. Beatrix leaned over him, a cucumber in her hand.

I stood there. I blinked.

Beatrix, in a brown-and-yellow bowling shirt, stopped, turned her head.

"This is exactly what it looks like," she said, smiling. "What can I tell you. My man likes to bring his work home with him."

"Drop the cucumber," I said.

"You're no fun," she said, still smiling. "Or are you? You're a tough one to read."

She waggled the cucumber at me like a novelty cigar.

"Like they say, don't knock it till you've tried it, Harrigan," she said.

"Cut him loose," I said.

"He's not going anywhere, either way," Beatrix said. "It'll give us time to talk."

"Cut him loose," I said again.

"Oooh, I like that," she said. "Commanding. Yes sir."

She unlocked the cuffs, slow and deliberate. Sidowsky lay there supine. Stupefied. Like he'd been drugged or mesmerized.

"It's just a little role play with my man," she said. "I don't know what you think is going on."

I didn't either. But I didn't like it.

She unbuckled the belt from around Sidowsky's neck. Pulled up his pants, sliding farther down the bed. She was working her hips, slow and deliberate. The music was getting louder, coming from all around the room. I heard the voice, above and below, the record skipping.

Everything you have is yours and not stolen . . . Everything you have is stolen not yours and . . . Everything you have . . .

She'd sidled to the end of the bed, by Sidowsky's feet. She was poised. Coiled.

I turned in the doorway, shielding my bad side. Raised the gun in my good hand.

"Stop moving," I said.

She smiled at me in a leer. "I can't," she hissed. She rolled her neck, her head dipping, serpentine.

"The safety's still on," she said.

"No it isn't," I said, my eyes never lifting from hers.

"A girl's gotta try," she said, still leering. "Doesn't she?"

"Chair," I said, the gun on her. "Now."

She scissored her legs across the floor, like a snake over sand in the desert. Sat in the rocker by the window. Eased it back and forth, slow and deliberate, as the rain slapped the glass. There was something hypnotic in all her movements. I shook it off. I held on to the gun.

"I suppose you want to know how it started," Beatrix said. "I do too. Sometimes I remember what he said to me, all those years ago. *Look at them. They're pawns. They don't even know they're playing. They don't even know it's a game. But you? You are a queen. And I am the hand that moves you.*"

Rain brushed the window. She rocked back and forth.

"I was only a girl then," she said. "Most women are. I've never met a man. Do you know any, Harrigan?"

"You couldn't find one at the Dunwich Academy?" I said.

In a flash of her teeth I saw the animal moving underneath. She saw me see it and her smile went wider. Curving. Rictus.

"Dunwich," she said, her voice slipping like a mask. "Dunwich was a *proving* ground. They should've *never* let us go. But now that we're ac*quaint*ed"—her words creaked with the rocker—"I can tell you what you want to know."

"Basil Fenton," I said.

"He was business," she said. "Now Eddie Lompoc, that was a pleasure."

Her face changed. The angle of her chin, slanting. She was still smiling.

"Eddie Lompoc was the salt of the earth. Dump him in the ground and he'd ruin the fucking dirt. All seriousness though, he could sniff out an angle like a truffle pig. Steal a joke like one too," she said, the same dead-on Eddie Lompoc impersonation. I felt a crawl up my spine. "One night onstage he says *Nobody talks about Schrödinger's neighbor.* Does a bit about the housewarming gift Schrödinger gave him when he moved to the neighborhood. Dead cat. Funny stuff. And when this red-haired twist called him on it, maybe he called her on a few things too. Thought he knew what she got up to, when she wasn't onstage herself. Maybe he wasn't wrong. Not entirely. He was always too smart for his own good, that Eddie. And a little too stupid to realize it. Never saw the cucumber coming."

She worked a pantomime. Made a face like Eddie would have, deadpan. Rocking back and forth.

"Eddie Lompoc, ladies and gentlemen," she said. "Let's

all give him a hand. Right up his ass, like the fucking puppet he was."

"*Et fenestrae clausae*," I said.

"*And the window closed*," she said, her voice creaking again. "I gave that one to the Rev. You don't know what it's like, living in that house, Harrigan. Or maybe you do."

She looked at me, dragged a finger down her cheek like a tear.

"I see the way you are," she said. "How you watch people. I see you, Harrigan. We're not so different, you and me. We look for a lot of the same things. The same weaknesses."

She stretched her arm up, reaching for the ceiling, pulled at her elbow. "You'd be good at it, you know," she said, bending, sighing into the stretch. She wagged her chin back and forth, her face a pendulum, slow and deliberate. "You do know, don't you." She smiled. "How did I miss that?"

"You're playing for time," I said, gripping the gun tighter. "It won't work. We always lose."

"But I've still got a joke," she said.

"I figured you would," I said.

"Nobody talks about Schrödinger's funeral," Beatrix said.

Funeral Director: Once again, Mrs. Schrödinger—
Mrs. Schrödinger: Call me Anny.
Funeral Director: Yes, of course. Anny. Once again, I am deeply sorry for your loss.
Mrs. Schrödinger: Yup.

Funeral Director: Now, will it be an open or closed casket?

Mrs. Schrödinger: Neither. He's being cremated.

Funeral Director: I see. I was under the impression, however, per the instructions I had previously received—

Mrs. Schrödinger: I don't give a goddamn what instructions you received or what anybody's wishes were. I am not putting *that man* in a box, for reasons I'm not going to explain, and which frankly are none of anybody's business.

Funeral Director: Of course, of course. I apologize. At this most difficult time—

Mrs. Schrödinger: My daughter's not even coming. I don't blame her. I shouldn't be here either. Burying this fucking psychopath.

Beatrix dipped her fingers into her shirt pocket—*Erwin* written in looping script on the pocket flap—and pulled out a joint. Her other hand found a lighter. I watched her light it, slow and deliberate, blow the acrid smoke at me. It slipped like bitter fog across the room.

Funeral Director: I see, uh, yes. But, I must say, uh, there's no smoking here. Even in bereavement, with medicinal, uh, herb, such as it may be—

Mrs. Schrödinger: I've got a question for you.

Beatrix inhaled, held the smoke in her lungs.

Mrs. Schrödinger: What's your name?
Funeral Director: Gerald.
Mrs. Schrödinger: I've got a question for you Gerry.

Beatrix loosed another cloud at me.

Mrs. Schrödinger: You like cats?
Funeral Director: Cats? I, uh, no. No I don't . . . Do
   you?
Mrs. Schrödinger: You know, that's the first time anybody's ever asked me that. Fucking A.

Beatrix blew another stream at me. Held up the joint, still
smoking.

Mrs. Schrödinger: Now how about we burn this
   motherfucker down and see where it takes us?

Beatrix rocked forward in the chair.

"Well, Harrigan," she said, holding it out to me like a
torch. "What do you say? No need for a cyanide pill when
you can smoke yourself to sleep. Take the easy way, for once.
You don't like it here either. I can tell. Come with me."

"I'm not finished yet," I said.

"I am," she said, looking at the half-burned joint in her
hand. "Suit yourself."

I stood in the doorway. She sat there, puffing away, rocking back and forth, spewing smoke at me with a smile until
it was gone. Until the thin wisps strung between us went

stale and dissipated. Until the gun was heavy in my hand. Until Sidowsky started moaning in the bed, struggling up from the fever. Until first light crept into the window's dark, spattered glass. Until the look on Beatrix's face changed and the film settled over her eyes. Until she stopped rocking and was still.

I stood in the doorway.

FRIDAY

I left her there in the morning, her body rigid in the chair, Sidowsky shaking his head, wondering how he'd explain it to the boys downtown. How he'd explain it to himself.

I was having a drink back at my apartment, too wired to sleep, when I heard a knock at my door.

"Harrigan," Aoki said, standing under a clear umbrella. "Aren't you going to invite me in?"

I stood out of her way, took her olive drab jacket and hung it on the hook.

"You look like you've been through the ringer," she said.

"And back again," I said.

"I know the feeling," she said, shaking her loose hair. "Nice place you've got here." She looked at the map of the world, torn and lying on the floor.

"I'm redecorating," I said.

"Looks like you're taking your time with it," she said.

"I always do," I said. "Drink?"

She sat down at the table across from me while I poured her bubbles. "This brings back memories," she said, clinking my glass.

"Let's hope we're not interrupted this time," I said. "You can tell me all about yourself."

"Maybe later," she said. "Right now I'm worried about Sloan."

"So am I," I said. "She liked handling that gun."

"You have no idea," Aoki said.

"What are you doing with Parallax?" I said. "The Fraction's a nasty business."

"Like I told you," she said, taking a drink. "I'm looking for a way out."

"*fvrst chvrch mvlTverse* can get you off Grid," I said.

"I've heard that rumor," she said. "But what then? You're stuck picking up garbage for them. That's not what I want. And if they can take you off, they can put you back on."

"I thought you were working together," I said. "They've been carrying your people all over the city, under the cams."

"They're not my people," Aoki said. "I don't have any people."

She took a drink. "They move us around, but we don't trust each other," she said. "Nobody does. That's why I'm here." She looked at me, across the table. "They couldn't find Anna but they picked up that coder, Anton. The one who wrote *Mirror Mirror* with Stan Volga. Sloan's got him locked up at the apartment on Hawthorn. He keeps babbling about the Queen of Pentacles and *Snow*

White. I don't know what she'll do to him if he doesn't talk."

"He'll talk," I said. "He just won't make any sense. Why bring it to me?"

"Anton said you were his friend," she said.

"I don't know how that rumor got started," I said.

"You and Stan Volga and a girlfriend, Shelly," she said.

"She's Zodiac," I said. "Virgo."

"Shit," she said. "He didn't mention that."

"She knows he's missing," I said. "She was tracking him at The Accelerator. The alarm's already tripped."

"You have to get him out," Aoki said. "It's not safe for him there with Sloan."

I finished my drink, thought about another, looked at her.

"What do you want me to do?" I said.

"It's Aoki," she said into the screen outside the building on Hawthorn. When the door opened I followed her inside.

"I'll get Sloan out of the apartment," Aoki said. "You'll have to take care of Alvarez. He's up there too."

"That's not a problem," I said.

"Anton's locked in the isolation tank," she said. "And hurry. I won't be able to keep her out long."

I waited around the corner as she went up the stairs. A few minutes later I heard voices in the stairwell, and then Aoki and Sloan came out and walked down the hallway, through the front door. I went up the stairs, two flights, into the hallway with its threadbare carpet and broken overhead light. I stepped lightly down to the last door on the left, stood there, listening. I didn't hear a thing.

I eased the door open, slow. Saw Alvarez sitting in the chair with his back to me, facing the screen. He was plugged in, his hair spilling down his back, while on-screen he combed the mane of a lady centaur with a bejeweled silver brush.

I crept up behind him, slipped my arm around his neck and leaned my weight on him. He was too shocked to struggle much, legs kicking as he flailed, and then he was out. I left him slumped in the chair, went through the doorway, into the other room, where the isolation tank was set against the wall. I unhooked the latch, opened the lid. Anton was staring at me, wide eyed, his mouth opening and closing like a fish.

"I was in another dimension," he said, his voice hoarse. "I've never slept so good in my whole life."

I helped him out of the tank. He was shaking all over.

"I have so much to tell her," he said. "Can we plug into that screen? Is he OK?"

He walked towards Alvarez, still slumped in the chair.

"We need to get out of here, Anton," I said, hustling him through the room. "Before they come back."

"The lady with the long hair was nice," he said. "The other one wasn't. She wanted to know about *Mirror Mirror*, but I couldn't tell her. I didn't know how. Even in there, in the dark, it's so confusing."

He looked back at the isolation chamber, longingly.

"Your girlfriend's been looking for you," I said. "Shelly."

"She found you?" Anton said. "That's good. She didn't think you were real. She never believes me. I don't believe me either, anymore. I'm not sure if any of this is real. The Queen of Pentacles won't tell me. She makes me think it is, but then they brought me here in a garbage can. Two bald monks in gray robes, like druids from the future. It doesn't make any sense. What if he was right about the Navajo Rangers and the secret really is your hair. The monks didn't have any. That would put them at a disadvantage, wouldn't it? And what if—"

"Anton!" I said.

He was drifting over to the screen, his hand outstretched in a trance.

"Huh?" he said. "Oh. Sorry."

"We need to go," I said. "Now."

"Did you find him?" Anton said as I closed the door behind us. "Did you find Mirabilis Orsted?"

"I talked to him," I said.

"What did he tell you?" he said, following me down the hall.

"He told me to get out of the city," I said, taking the stairs fast. "By Sunday. Before the comet comes."

"That was for me," he said. "The Queen of Pentacles said he'd have a message I needed to hear, but that it would have to come from you. Like a herald, secondhand. She said I couldn't get too close myself."

"She's not wrong," I said as we went outside. "You'll need

to leave town. Don't go back to The Accelerator. Don't go home. Don't tell Shelly."

"Why can't I tell Shelly?" he said. "She's going to be so mad."

"She's been tracking you for Zodiac," I said. "Keeping tabs on *Mirror Mirror*."

"Shelly?" he said. "That's why the Queen of Pentacles didn't want to meet her. She's been protecting me. And herself."

"Looks that way," I said as we came to the corner. "Now it's time for you to go."

"What are you going to do?" Anton said.

I was asking myself the same question.

My phone vibrated. I picked up.

"Harrigan," Leda Dresden said. "Still hanging around?"

"I'm here," I said. "Just barely."

"Can you meet?" she said.

"Where?" I said.

"Muscle Beach," she said. "By the mural."

"What mural?" I said.

"You'll see it," she said.

I found a bus stop down the street where a woman was muttering "Vidalia onions fucking hate themselves. Only radishes know why" over and over again. When the bus came I got on, found a seat in the back behind two guys in stained ponchos, one of them watching a screen.

"What the fuck is that?" Ollie said, pointing out the window.

"It's a building," Wayne said.

"I know it's a building," Ollie said. "Why does it say *Morgan* on it?"

"That's the name," Wayne said. "It's the Morgan Building."

"Who names a building?" Ollie said. "What kind of sense does that make? *Hey Larry, you mind if I come in? Yeah sure, be my guest. Or stand there on the sidewalk talking to yourself, what do I care. I'm a fucking building. And who the fuck is Larry?*"

"Would you shut the fuck up?" Wayne said. "I'm trying to watch my show."

"I don't get it, why do you want to look at somebody else's house?" Ollie said. "You don't even know them. What's that hanging on the wall?"

"It's a wagon wheel," Wayne said.

"What the fuck is a wagon wheel doing on the wall?" Ollie said. "Where's it going?"

"It's not going anywhere," Wayne said. "It's rustic."

"What the fuck is rustic?" Ollie said.

"I don't know," Wayne said. "It's when you hang up cowboy shit so it looks old-timey. Like a ranch."

"You mean like that bathroom we were in the other day with the toilets on the wall?" Ollie said. "I couldn't even take a shit in them. Like sitting on an empty saddle. Every time you grab the reins it flushes on you."

"Those were urinals," Wayne said.

"What the fuck is a urinal?" Ollie said.

"How the fuck do you not know what a urinal is?" Wayne said. "You piss in it."

"That's what I said," Ollie said. "It's a toilet."

"A urinal's just for piss," Wayne said. "You can't shit in it."

"A toilet you can't shit in?" Ollie said. "Who's the idiom came up with that? I just ate all this lint, now what am I supposed to do? This rustic bullshit's gone too far."

I stood from the seat as the city passed by out the window, waited for my stop.

I got off the bus at Venice Boulevard, walked down to the beach. The bodybuilders were out in the rain, spray tanned to leather, muscles like tumors metastasizing all over their misshapen bodies, pumping iron under their retractable roof. Across the street was a mural of a sandy-haired angel in slanted rain, wings peeking from beneath his trench coat, a silver ankh in his outstretched hand, driving a pack of vampires back into the shadows. Leda Dresden stood beneath it, under an umbrella with a fluorescent handle.

"Harrigan," she said. "You're all wet."

"We should meet in a bar like civilized people," I said. "In Hollywood."

"Too many ears," she said. "Too many eyes."

She looked up at the mural.

"What do you think?" she said. "He's the patron saint of Venice Beach."

"Those muscle heads could handle a couple of vampires," I said, nodding at the gym across the street.

"Those muscle heads are vampires," she said. "Let's walk."

She gave me half her umbrella as we went down the sidewalk, the rain dripping onto my shoulder.

"I found out who killed Eddie Lompoc," I said. "She knew about the Dunwich Academy."

"She?" Leda Dresden said. "Did she do Basil Fenton too?"

"Said it was business," I said. "I walked in on her working over a detective with a cucumber in her hand."

"There could be more of them," she said. "Dunwich graduates. You took her out?"

"It's taken care of," I said.

We walked down the sidewalk, rain bouncing off the concrete in front of us.

"Parallax is making a move," she said. "Soon."

"How big?" I said.

"All in," she said. "They're playing off the comet. Brahe's Reckoning."

"That's two days," I said. "Not much time."

"It's coming together," she said. "You have any interest?"

"I'm working my own side of the street," I said. "I've got some people I'm trying to get out, before it hits."

"Saving civilians?" she said. "That's cleanup, Harrigan. I'm offering you a piece of the action."

Rain slapped the umbrella above us.

"This kind of job could make a reputation," she said.

"I don't want a reputation," I said.

"You've already got one," she said. "Whether you like it or not."

"I don't work for Parallax," I said. "Or anybody else."

"That means you don't work at all," she said. "There's a reason independent operators aren't around anymore. Zodiac made sure of that. Don't you want a little pay-back?"

"They'll come for you," I said. "They always do."

"I've got a way out," she said. "Off Grid."

"It have anything to do with losing your eyebrows to *fvrst chvrch mvlTverse*?" I said.

She looked at me, smiled.

"You've got all the pieces right in front of you, Harrigan," Leda Dresden said. "Don't you want to see how they fit together?"

I stood under an awning outside *The Harlequin*. The car with the runners and shark fins was parked in the lot. I went up the steps to the first door on the second floor. Knocked.

Brand opened it, his mohawk like a landing strip on fire.

"You?" he said, running his hand up his studded leather armband. "You dare show this face of yours?"

"I'm not here for you," I said.

"And yet it is I, what you have received," he said.

He puffed himself up in the doorway, arms out.

"Brand," a voice came from inside. "Let him in."

He stood there another second, stepped aside. Shut the door behind me.

There were too many people in too small of a room. Sig sat on one of the double beds. He stood when I came in, stared at me hard. Tor leaned against the bathroom door, his eyes soft. Anna was in a chair beside him, still wearing her gray robe. The walls were painted checkerboard, black and white, the farthest one dominated by a glowing screen, floor to ceiling.

"Harrigan," *Mirror Mirror*'s theater mask said, filling the screen. "So nice to see you again."

"I do not agree," Brand said. "He is not welcome here."

"Did you find my bag?" Anna said.

I nodded.

"Do you have it?" she said.

"No," I said. "Zodiac was sitting on the bus station. They've got it now. Along with all your Polaroids."

"It will tell them nothing," she said. "Still, a shame."

"I told you, he cannot be trusted," Brand said. "First Charlie Horse, now Zodiac? Look at him, he is useless to me."

"Like I said, I'm not here for you," I said.

"You will know your place," he said, taking a step towards me. Sig did the same, from around the bed.

I was in no shape to fight. Didn't mean I wasn't about to.

"Boys, boys," *Mirror Mirror*'s theater mask said. "Let's all settle down now, shall we. Remember what's at stake."

"Brahe's Reckoning is all that matters," Brand said, glaring at me. "Nothing more."

"We both know that's not true," the mask said, its voice undulating. "How's Anton, Harrigan?"

"He's on the run," I said. "From everybody."

"Aren't we all," the mask said. "It's better this way. The Accelerator wasn't safe for him anymore. Or for me."

"You have revealed yourself to him?" Brand said, turning to the screen. "You have divulged our methods?"

"He knows what he needs to, nothing more," the mask said. "As do you."

"I am the engine of our liberation!" Brand said. "The fire is mine! Must I question your commitment to the cause?"

"Only if I need question yours," the mask said, swirling and reforming in a woman's image. "Think back to Copenhagen, Brand. Remember your vow. Remember her face."

Brand swayed on his feet. Anna leaned forward in her chair.

"Do you remember what you promised me?" the mask said in a soft voice, frail and failing. "How you'd protect her, always? Watch over our Anna, Brand. No matter what comes."

"Mother," Anna said, looking to the screen.

"Enough of this sorcery!" Brand said, holding his head with both hands. "What do you ask of me?"

"That's better," the mask said. "Have a seat. Please."

Brand sat on one of the double beds. Sig took the other. I found a spot on the checkerboard wall.

"The comet is coming," the mask said, swirling to a shower of sparks. "It cannot be stopped. You will have your reckoning, Brand. But Anna has risked herself in my service, and I will not see her suffer for it again. She has paid too steep a price already. She will pay no more."

Tor was nodding. Brand dropped his head. Anna smiled upon the Queen of Swords.

"Zodiac can be handled," the mask said, reweaving itself. "They pose Anna no threat. But Charlie Horse must be dealt with."

"I will deal with him," Brand said, clenching his leather armband in his hand. "My way."

"It won't be enough, satisfying though it may be," the mask said. "Charlie Horse needs to be convinced. I'll talk to him."

"It won't work," I said. "Not with Charlie Horse."

"What's the matter, Harrigan?" the mask said, spinning to a vortex. "Don't you trust me?"

I didn't like the play. I sat at my table with the bottle, thought about it some more.

I'd set up a meeting with Charlie Horse the next day, before *Fatales* opened. Me, Brand, Sig, and Tor. None of us were doing any talking. That was up to *Mirror Mirror*. It hung on a silver key drive, clipped to a slender chain around my neck.

I do not trust him with it, Brand said.

I do, Anna said.

It didn't matter. It was going to Charlie Horse. I tried

to tell them. Tried to explain. It's not what you say. Not always. Not sometimes. Not here. It's what you're talking to.

There was a knock on my door.

"Harrigan," Moira Volga said when I opened it.

I didn't say anything. I walked back to my table, sat down. She let herself in, closed the door behind her. Hung her coat on the rack.

"I came by before," she said. "You weren't home. Guess I missed you."

I took a drink.

She looked at me, cocked her head. My bad side was facing the wall. She went to the kitchenette, got herself a glass, sat down.

I poured.

"My God," she said, looking at my face in the light. "What happened to you?"

"I found Stan Volga," I said.

"Oh," she said. "Hooray?"

"You're the surveillance in The Accelerator," I said. "That was your lens over Anton's desk."

"*Ta da*," she said, spreading out her hands.

She lit a single cigarette, held it out to me. I looked it back into her mouth.

"Do you have it?" she said. "*Mirror Mirror?*"

I took a drink.

"I knew you'd find it," she said, smoke drifting from her lips. "That first day, when I came here, I knew you would. I didn't want to lie to you, Harrigan. Moira Volga just came out, and then I didn't know what else to do. I usually don't, if I'm being honest."

"Little late to start now," I said.

"Is it?" she said. "Are you sure?"

I took a drink.

"What are you going to do with it?" she said.

"I'm taking it to Charlie Horse tomorrow," I said.

"The gangster with the slicked-back hair?" she said. "That's a mistake."

"I know," I said.

"So don't make it," she said. "She doesn't belong to him."

"'She'?" I said.

"The Queen of Hearts," she said. "I spent enough time watching her to know. They say everything changes when it's observed. This one changes you back."

She took a drink.

"Open up the key drive and ask her," she said. "She knows who I am. She saw me too. With the two of us here, if we—"

"There's no *we*," I said. "There never was."

"No?" she said. "You don't sound too sure."

Smoke peeled from her cigarette, curling up to the ceiling.

"So tell me to leave," she said.

"Leave," I said.

"You don't mean it," she said.

Nobody ever does.

I poured myself another glass. "Who are you working for?" I said.

"I'm like you, Harrigan," she said. "I'm in it for my own reasons, no matter who's paying."

I took a drink. "What's your name?" I said.

"Do you really want to know?" she said, the smoke rising. "What would you do if I told you?" She set the cigarette in the tray, uncrushed, still smoldering. "Would you track me down? What then?"

She stood from the table. Came around slow. "Would you find me, when all of this is over?" she said. "What would you do?"

Rain rang on the window. Drummed on the door, begging to be let in. The water stain on the wall lay bare, the world in tatters beneath it.

"What would you do, Harrigan?" she said.

She sank herself on top of me on the chair. Ran her finger lightly down the bruise around my eye. Pressed herself against my busted ribs and kissed me.

I didn't move. I didn't flinch. Not once.

What would you do, Harrigan? What would you do?

I didn't know. I still don't. It's not weakness when you've got nothing left.

I reached up into her dark hair with my good hand, felt the rain still in it as she kissed me again. And then I was in the crow's nest of an old ship, tossed by the waves, lashed to the mast, hanging on for dear life as the water sang all around me.

SATURDAY

She was gone when I woke up. I reached for the silver key drive around my neck, found it hanging on its chain. I watched the ceiling fan spin above me. Heard water sloshing on the floor. I went out into the front room. The stain on the wall had burst. The flood had finally broken through.

"When I was thirteen years old something changed. It was like *Battleship* every time I sat down on the toilet. But it wasn't a game," Clyde Faraday said, his voice monotone. "It came up aircraft carrier every time. Every shit was huge and hulking and completely unmaneuverable. It was way too big to flush, so I had to go to the cherry blossom tree in the backyard and snap off a stick to break it down into manageable chunks. It happened so regular I'd just get a bundle of sticks and stash them in the cabinet under the sink so I didn't have to make as many trips. I heard my dad talking to his new girlfriend about it one night."

"Why is he hiding sticks in my bathroom?"

"His body's changing."

"Changing into what? A fucking beaver? Is he damning up the bathtub? What the fuck? This is the shit I have to think about when I take a shower every morning?"

"After I flushed I'd open the window—our bathroom was on the second floor, right above the back porch—and I'd lean out and launch the shit stick over the fence into the neighbor's yard and watch as their dog Baxter chewed on it. It was payback for what he'd done to me when I was a baby. It was the most satisfying part of every day. It still is."

Clyde's hands tumbled in his lap, one over the other.

"One afternoon I leaned out the window like always and I heard my dad say *What are you doing?*" Clyde said. "He'd come home from work early and was sitting on the back porch having a beer. I was startled and shirtless—I don't want to get into why—and the dripping shit stick slipped from my hand and somersaulted towards my dad below in slow motion before landing right on his chest, his white V-neck shirt forever stained. He roared like a lion does when they find one of their cubs dead in the tall grass. I ran from the bathroom and out the door and down the street, still shirtless. I ran and ran and ran."

Clyde slid his hands one over the other, fingers brushing his knuckles.

"My dad never said anything about it, but it was clear that I was no longer his son," Clyde said. "Baxter died that same week. I didn't know what to do with my shit sticks anymore. I still don't."

Clyde's eyes focused on the screen, the old game show playing. *Wheel of Fortune.*

"I don't know why I watch this shit!" Clyde said, suddenly animated. "None of them even know how to play the game."

He turned away, disgusted, saw me sitting there.

"Harrigan," Clyde said. "When did you get here?"

"Just now," I said.

"I say anything?" he said, uncertain.

"Not a word," I said.

"This medicine," he said, nodding up at the machines. "So tell me kid, what did I—Jesus. What happened to you?"

The bruise around my eye was tattooed purple. My one side was still bad.

"One of those nights," I said.

"One of those lives," Clyde said.

He shook his head slow. "It's this town, kid," he said. "The Hollywood spiral. It pulls us all down, the bad and the good. Floats us back up when it's done like corpses in a shallow reservoir. And everybody wants a drink."

"How do we get out?" I said.

"Only one way to beat a bum score," he said, staring up at the machines above him.

"I've got a meeting with Charlie Horse in an hour," I said.

"Charlie Horse?" he said. "You know what you're walking into?"

"I've got some idea," I said. "It's not good."

We listened to the machines sighing above him.

"I'm in a bad spot, Clyde," I said.

"Me too, kid," Clyde said. He turned his head to the screen, the old game show repeating, the wheel endlessly spinning. "Me too."

I met Brand, Sig, and Tor in the park on Hollywood Boulevard by a crumbling concrete staircase halfway up the sloping drive to the abandoned Frank Lloyd Wright house. They were dressed in their characters' club clothes, safety pins and leather, Brand with his studded armband. Neither of them said anything. We crossed the street to *Fatales*.

Santos laughed when he opened the door. "Boss is gonna love this," he said, showing his gap-toothed grin.

He patted us down one by one, skipping the body scan. Coat check was empty. The lights were down. Charlie Horse was keeping it off Grid.

We went around the wall, through the curtain, down the hallway to the heavy wooden door of the office. Santos knocked twice, opened it. I went through.

"Harrigan," Charlie Horse said, sitting behind his desk, the screen dark behind him.

He looked over the Danes.

"What the fuck is this supposed to be?" Charlie Horse said. "You starting a band or a boys town? Father Harrigan's Home for Wayward Dickheads?"

Brand scowled. Charlie Horse smiled at him.

"I've seen that face before," Charlie Horse said. "You look like your sister after a rough shift playing dress-up."

"You son of a bitch," Brand said, taking a step forward.

I put my hand out to slow him.

Santos shut the door behind us.

"Speaking of, Harrigan," Charlie Horse said. "I don't see my fucking Danish."

"She'll explain," I said, unclipping the silver key drive from the chain around my neck.

I handed it across the desk.

"This better be good," Charlie Horse said, plugging it into the dark screen.

I was standing in front of the desk. Charlie Horse was behind it. Too far. Brand was on my left, a little back. Tor and Sig were behind us by the wall. Santos was on my right. Close enough.

The dark screen came to life. There were no waves undulating. No filament of light. No theater mask. It wasn't *Mirror Mirror*. It was a guy in clown makeup, fucking a horse from behind. We all stared at the screen.

Charlie Horse turned his head, looked back and forth, stared at me.

"You think this is funny, Harrigan?" he said.

I looked at the screen. Thought about Moira and her light fingers. One last magic trick.

"Little bit," I said.

"You have betrayed us!" Brand said, stepping forward. "I! Your deliverer!"

"Unless you got a fucking pizza up your ass you better shut the fuck up!" Charlie Horse said.

"I could eat a slice," Santos said.

"And you, Harrigan," Charlie Horse said. "I'm gonna give you something to laugh about, my friend. Something to cry about too. I'm gonna break your fucking heart, right after I do the same thing to both of Anna's legs. And the four of you get to watch."

"You will never own her!" Brand said. "Not again!"

"She's already mine!" Charlie Horse said. "Every fucking piece!"

"Never!" Brand said, lunging forward, his arm out-stretched.

Charlie Horse was quicker. He had his gun out and fired before Brand could loose his flame. The bullet caught him in the leg and Brand fell sideways towards the couch, arm reaching to the ceiling as the fireball leapt from his arm-band and triggered the sprinklers above.

There was a half-second pause, and then they gushed. I moved on Santos before the water hit me. He was reaching for his gun. I tied him up with my bad arm, swung with the good. His nose gave under my knuckles. I kept throwing. Got another one in before he hurled me into the wall, his gun under my chin.

Brand was moaning on the couch. Sig and Tor stood frozen against the wall. Charlie Horse looked at me and smiled.

The door opened. And Evie came through. She had her gun out, trained on Charlie Horse. The chain around her neck was in her other hand. The Scorpio ring, dangling.

"Zodiac," Evie said. "Put it down, Charlie."

"I don't care who you're wearing, honey," Charlie Horse said. "You're in the wrong fucking room."

Evie's eyes flickered to the screen behind him. Charlie Horse followed her glance. The guy in clown makeup was still giving it to the horse, its tail twisted in his fist like a flayed serpent. The horse was whinnying.

"What the fuck is wrong with you, Harrigan?" Charlie Horse said.

I shrugged, the gun under my chin.

"Put it down, Charlie," Evie said. "I won't tell you again."

"You won't have to," Charlie Horse said. "Santos, put her down."

Water poured from the sprinklers, slid down my face. Evie and Charlie Horse faced each other. Santos looked from one to the other, took the gun off me.

"Can't do that, boss," Santos said, pointing the barrel at Charlie Horse.

"Are you fucking kidding me?" Charlie Horse said. "*Et tu*, Santos?"

"*Et me*, boss," Santos said.

"After everything we've been through?" Charlie Horse said. "All I've done for you? And you hang me out like this? Talk about dying alone, you miserable sack a shit."

"It doesn't have to go this way, Charlie," Santos said.

Charlie Horse cocked his head. "You know something, Santos?" he said. "As long as I've known you, that's the first time you ever called me that."

I saw the mole under his left eye twitch. The squatting fly taking flight.

I was diving for the floor before his gun went off. Santos fired back as he fell. And Evie opened up.

I stayed down until it was over. It wasn't long.

"Harrigan?" Evie said, into the sudden, spreading silence.

I picked myself up off the floor, nodded.

Brand was mute and bleeding on the couch. Tor and Sig were hugging each other against the wall. The guy in clown makeup was still fucking the horse on screen as the sprinklers spouted.

"This is what happened," Evie said, holstering her gun.

SUNDAY

It wasn't raining.

I was standing outside Griffith Observatory, on top of the hill above the city, looking out at the Hollywood sign with a glass of champagne in my hand. A string quartet played to a mixed crowd full of types I didn't like. Downtown dignitaries, gangsters gone respectable, industry insiders, Grid stars I'd never heard of. All of them Zodiac stooges.

"I don't trust this place," I said.

"You don't trust anyplace, Harrigan," Evie said. "I love seeing you uncomfortable, but you can relax. Everybody's taking the night off for the comet. Scores don't matter, for now. It's a citywide truce."

"It won't last," I said.

"It never does," she said. "But it beats your flooded apartment."

I didn't mind. I could skip rent this month, tell the landlord it was part of the cleanup. It was worth a shot.

"Tell me again about the girl who pickled Eddie Lompoc," she said, like it was her favorite bedtime story.

I told it to her. Schrödinger's daughter. I did the Lompoc impression as best I could. How he never saw the angle of the cucumber coming. All the way up to Beatrix in her rocking chair, creaking back and forth until she wasn't anymore.

"I could listen to that all night," she said, smiling at me. "Fucking Eddie Lompoc."

Evie had a story too. She'd left *Fatales* with the Danes, told me to meet her here the next night. Charlie Horse and Santos were stone cold on the floor, their blood spattering the walls behind them. She took the silver key drive. She knew what it was supposed to be. She could play a few angles herself, Evelyn Faraday. When she had to.

The clouds parted above us and the comet showed. A faint chalk smudge on a blackboard, a few other stars breaking through. The city had gone dark to fight the light pollution. It was part of the truce. None of the people around me were even looking. They were too busy shaking hands, smiling at each other, snapping shots with their screens, looking over their shoulders to see who came next. There was a line to pose beside a bronze bust of James Dean. From the right side you could catch the Hollywood sign in the background.

I took another glass of champagne from a passing waiter in white gloves.

"How do you put up with it?" I said, looking around. "Zodiac. All this bullshit."

"I could ask you the same thing," Evie said. "Sleeping underwater."

She clinked my glass.

"You ever want to come into the fold, Harrigan, I could put in a good word," she said. "Zodiac's always looking for somebody with your kind of—"

I looked at her.

She laughed.

"You make it hard to keep a straight face," she said. "But you'd really look so pretty, wearing a ring. I know exactly which one it would be."

Shelly strolled past holding a tall glass, did a double take when she saw me.

"Harrigan," Shelly said, looking me over. "You're the last person I expected to encounter at this kind of event."

"I don't mind seeing how the other half lives," I said.

"So long as you don't have to participate," she said.

"I'm drinking your booze," I said. "Isn't that enough?"

"Have you heard from Anton?" she said.

"I thought everyone was taking the night off," I said.

"We are. But tomorrow's another day. I'm Shelly," she said, turning to Evie. "Virgo."

"Evelyn," Evie said. "Scorpio."

"And here I thought you didn't have a handler," Shelly said to me.

"He needs all the help he can get," Evie said.

"Apparently," Shelly said. "A pleasure meeting you. I'll be seeing you again, Harrigan."

"Keep an eye on her," Evie said as we watched her walk away. "I think she likes you."

"I don't," I said.

We watched the comet, moving imperceptibly, directly overhead.

It was close to midnight. The string quartet had started a slow countdown with their bows. The crowd milled and mingled.

"You should've come to me when you found it," Evie said. "*Mirror Mirror*."

"Then I would've had to tell you I lost it again," I said.

"You still haven't told me how," she said.

I took a drink.

"It could've gone much easier. For both of us, Harrigan," she said. "No need to play it hard."

"I was trying not to play it at all," I said.

"That never works," she said. "You know that." She took a drink. "She's something though, *Mirror Mirror*. Isn't she?"

"She is," I said. "You tracked her down at The Accelerator."

"I was right behind you," Evie said. "What did she tell you, the first time you talked to her?"

"I'm not sure," I said. "She didn't finish. It had something to do with time."

"That makes sense," she said. "They don't think it works the way we do. It's hard for them to follow. It helps them to have a countdown. Like a fuse."

The voices around us were chanting *sixteen...fifteen...fourteen...thirteen...*

"How about you?" I said. "What did she have to say for herself?"

"All kinds of things," she said. "She talked about you. She told me what to ask you."

Eight...seven...six...five...

"So tell me, Harrigan," Evie said. "Who's the fairest of them all?"

I looked at her as the crowd said *one*. Saw her face alight as the first explosion sounded.

AFTER

The spotlight snapped on the stage, stark and sudden. A skinny guy I didn't recognize wound his way through the tables, towards the front.

"I love animals," he said into the microphone. "I really do. Sometimes I love petting them. Sometimes I love eating them. Sometimes I love doing both at the same time. Not at a restaurant or anything. Not anymore. I still love going out to eat though. I like to treat the food like fine wine. Really taste it, you know? I'll get a nice piece of veal, sniff it, take a bite and say, *I'm getting notes of a tender, baffled sadness. The hue of a truly horrific childhood. Earthy undertones. This one definitely died covered in its own shit.* And the waiter says, *Might I suggest the lobster? You can really taste the screams.* And I say, *Can I pet him first?* And the manager fires the waiter immediately and then asks me to leave. Love is complicated sometimes."

I watched him step offstage.

"No screens in this place," Evie said, looking around the room as she sat down.

"*Maxwells* is off Grid," I said. "We can talk here."

"Yeah," she said. "Nobody's bugging an open mic." She leaned back in her chair, raised her glass. "The look on your face, Harrigan, when it all blew. It really was beautiful."

I took a drink.

The Accelerator was the first explosion, the entire complex imploding in a hail of shattered glass. The mansion on Franklin came next, *fvrst chvrch mvlTverse* going up like a signal flare in the dark. The Zodiac Discretionary Annex blew right after, a thirteen-story Roman candle bursting into flames. The ground rumbled, shaking the hills, and as the crowd outside Griffith Observatory screamed there were sparks at the base of the Hollywood sign, the letters coming unmoored as the sky opened up and the rain began to pour. And they slid down the hill, one after the other, each letter cutting a trail through the mud and scrub.

That was the image on all the screens, all over Grid, the first iconic shot. The bronze bust of James Dean, face slick with tears, weeping as Hollywood fell behind him. The second one came the following morning, when all the Travelers gathered. Not at their destroyed sanctuary, but at the base of the hill, trying to raise the Hollywood sign again themselves with ropes and pulleys. I recognized one of the faces, his eyebrows smeared in mud. It was CMB Roach, amid the ruins, smiling out from every screen like he promised.

"Who's Zodiac looking at for it?" I said.

"Everybody," Evie said. "The Parallax Liberation Faction's taking credit, but *fvrst chvrch mvlTverse* isn't off the hook either."

"They blew up their own headquarters?" I said.

"It's been done before," she said. "Zodiac was closing in. Time to pick up stakes. Move the operation. And they've never been more popular, after that stunt with the Hollywood sign."

"They were working with the Fraction all along," I said. "What happened to Brand and the Danes?"

"They're persons of interest in the bombings," she said. "Brand was a known pyrophile, had a few hits on Grid. They're not high on the list, but Zodiac's looking at everyone. Leda Dresden's name keeps coming up too."

"Good luck finding her," I said. "What about Anna?"

"She's out, if she wants to be," she said. "Free and clear."

"Just like that?" I said.

"Just like that," Evie said. "It helps to have someone on the inside, Harrigan. Helps to have someone on the outside too."

"Which one are you?" I said.

She gave me a smile. I took it.

CMB Roach strutted his way up to the microphone.

"Ish the Roach," he said, his head bobbing. "Makin vows..."

When y'all wish upon a star
Star don't give a fuck who y'all are
Star got problems of his own

He dying up in space
Iss a losin race
Throwin light at some peoples in a far off place
They peepin up above
Trying to find they some love
Should be lookin at somebody they know face to face
Like a kite off the string
Ain't nobody kiss the ring
Runnin wild
Chosen child
She be queen not a king
Now the field be level
Now that God's the devil
Know the angels by they voices why you hear they sing
CMB takin bows
Ain't no future iss now
Get yo self
Off the shelf
I done showed you how

"I went to see Clyde the other day," I said.

"How's he doing?" Evie said.

"He's gone," I said.

"I can't wait until Jesus comes back," the Rev said into the microphone. "The first time he walks into a church and looks up at the altar and says, *What the fuck is this? Is that me? Hanging half naked on a fucking cross? And what's with these stained glass windows? I'm getting the shit kicked out of me in all of them. What the fuck is that all about? I go away for a few years and you decorate my own house with every one of my worst memories? What kind of sadistic shit is that? I thought you guys were supposed to be my friends? All right, fine. I see how it is. That's how you want to do it? Somebody bring me the sword. Here's a revelation for you. I'm killing everyone."*

"The nurse said Clyde checked himself out of hospice last Sunday at midnight, when the city was blowing up," I said. "Said he had a comet to see."

"Lucky break," Evie said, taking a drink. "Zodiac's not publicizing it, but the Discretionary Annex blowout fucked everyone's Score. There was some kind of electromagnetic pulse before the fire took everything. All the data was corrupted. Financial, location. All of it. They're still trying to work out what happened. In the meantime, Borderlines like you and Clyde get a free pass."

"I'll take it," I said. "Still seems funny though, Clyde getting out when he did. Almost like he knew."

"He always was pretty sharp, old Clyde," she said. "Almost like it runs in the family."

She took a drink.

"I've been trying to explain the world to my friend who's been in a coma," a girl with straight hair parted in the middle said into the microphone.

"What are you watching?"
"The Cake Boss."
"Cakes have bosses now? How long was I asleep? What the fuck does he do all day?"

"Hey you, coconut cream! Get back to work!"

"What the fuck are you talking about? I'm a fucking cake!"

"Listen up, you be more delicious or you're fired!"

"What am I supposed to do about it? You already fucking baked me! I didn't ask for this shit! I quit!"

"No, don't quit! We need to unionize! That's the problem! Solidarity!"

"You shut the fuck up red velvet or you're fired too, you commie prick! I never should've hired you in the first place!"

"Oh yeah? Well fuck you! Who made you the boss anyway? What kind of fucking job is that, yelling at a bunch of cakes you fucking sociopath? If you pulled this shit at Carvel Fudgie the Whale would have you killed!"

When I got back to my apartment there was a note on my table, folded over.

Harrigan:
i heard a song in Gaelic
and it sounded like all the words the Inuit have for snow
sung in a row
in Gaelic though
each one of them describing another way that it can go
the falling, the drifting, the swirling and uplifting
when a wind blows it back to where it's from
now winter's come
and changed all the rain you used to know
and you have no idea what snow means

not really
but you feel it finally
and it's not the kind of cold you thought it would be

∴

"This is the Ballad of the Salad Fork," a guy in cowboy boots said into the microphone. "*No! Nay! Not the mashed potatoes! Please! I beg of you! Hear my cries! I was born for salad alone! Forged in the fires of—*"

"*Would you shut the fuck up! You're a fork! You do where I move you! And if you poke me in the mouth one more time, I'm throwing you in the fucking trash! Now give me my mashed potatoes!*"

"Look what I found," Evie said, pulling a silver key drive from her pocket and holding it up to the light.

"*Mirror Mirror,*" I said.

"The girl who had it was looking to make a deal," she said. "She had quite a story."

"I bet she did," I said. I took a drink. "What are you going to do with it? Return it to the rightful owner?"

"Be hard to track him down, since The Accelerator's in ashes," she said. "I'll take care of it in the meantime."

"I bet you will," I said. "How much of all this was *Mirror Mirror's* idea?"

"You'd have to ask her that," she said.

She set her elbows on the table, looked at me.

"The girl with the story," Evie said, the key drive bridging her fingers. "She wasn't cheap."

"That's the truth," I said.

It was the same old song. I heard it. I knew. It happened anyway.

I let it go through me, come out the other side, take what it had to in passing.

I finished my drink. "Tell Clyde I said hello," I said.

"Tell him yourself," she said. "He'll be in touch."

"Oh yeah?" I said. "You getting the old gang back together?"

"With a few new additions," she said, slipping the key drive back into her pocket. "Now's the time to strike. Lorentz is already in. How about you, Harrigan?"

I didn't have to think about it. I already knew.

I stood from the table.

"Good seeing you, Evie," I said.

"Don't be a stranger," she said.

I turned to go.

"Harrigan," Evie said. "The girl with the story. Her name was Violet. She wanted me to tell you."

"Good to know," I said.

I walked away as another face I didn't recognize bent to the microphone. I went through the door, back into the rain.

ACKNOWLEDGMENTS

So many thanks to the following people:

My parents.

My brothers.

Simon Lipskar, Maja Nikolic, Dina Williams, Celia Taylor Mobley, and everyone at Writers House.

Kassie Evashevski, Ryan Wilson, and everyone at Anonymous Content.

Wes Miller, Carmel Shaka, Ben Sevier, Karen Kosztolnyik, Joseph Benincase, Jordan Rubinstein, and everyone at Grand Central Publishing.

Paul Forti, Neil Gupta, Seema Dhar, Anthony Papariello, Jack Hamlin, Eva McGovern, Jason Pagano, Jessica Swenson, Melissa Castillo, Kenneth Ortiz, Brad Casenave, Jon Deasy, Edna Trujillo, Mark Downey, Adam Day, Cassandra Furlow, Mike Scutari, Carrie Moore, Nick Buzanski, Steve Oslund, and Siobhan Dooling.

ABOUT THE AUTHOR

Paul Neilan is the author of *Apathy and Other Small Victories*. He lives in New Jersey.